*Mercier Press is the oldest independent Irish
publishing house and has published books in the
fields of history, literature, folklore, music, art,
humour, drama, politics, current affairs, law
and religion. It was founded in 1944 by John
and Mary Feehan.*

*In the building up of a country
few needs are as great as that of a publishing
house which would make the people proud of
their past, and proud of themselves as a people
capable of inspiring and supporting a world of
books which was their very own. Mercier Press
has tried to be that publishing house. On the
occasion of our fiftieth anniversary we thank
the many writers and readers who have
supported us and contributed to our success.*

*We face our second half-century
with confidence.*

# FAVOURITE IRISH STORIES

*Selected by*

## ANTHONY BLUETT

MERCIER PRESS

**Mercier Press,**
PO Box 5, 5 French Church Street, Cork
16 Hume Street, Dublin 2

© Contributors

ISBN 1 85635 083 5

*A CIP is available of this book from the British Library.*

10 9 8 7 6 5 4 3 2

Printed in Ireland by Colour Books.

# Contents

Preface                                                             7

**Part One: The Writers**                                           9

From *Men Withering*: Francis MacManus                             10

*The Black Chafer*: Padraic Pearse                                 21

*The White Goat*: Seamus O'Kelly                                   25

*The Return*: Daniel Corkery                                       33

*The Awakening*: Pádraic Ó Conaire                                 43

*Daddo's Shilling*: Sigerson Clifford                              47

*Death Be Not Proud*: John B. Keane                                51

*The Horse Thieves of Ballysaggert*: Brian Cleeve                  60

**Part Two: The Story Tellers**                                    75

From *The Tailor and Ansty*: Eric Cross                            76

*After Hours*: Eamon Kelly                                        110

*Tobacco*: Eamon Kelly                                            116

*The Drink of Gold*: Kate Ahern                                   121

*The Pig-Headed Child*: Kate Ahern                                123

*The Proud Girl*: Kate Ahern                                      125

*The Feet-water*: Michael Dawson                                  126

# Preface

This volume is being published to mark the Fiftieth Anniversary of the Mercier Press, founded in 1944. The primary aim of the selection is to offer the reader an absorbing and entertaining book of stories. At the same time, a special effort has been made to include material that can be seen as typical of what the Mercier Press has put into print over the last half century. Along with undoubted classics of Irish literature, the reader will find pieces that belong to the popular tradition of storytelling.

Part One of this book brings together crucial figures such as Francis MacManus, Padraic Pearse and Daniel Corkery. The range of tone is wide, from Pearse's mystic allegories to MacManus' realistic historical drama. A lighter note is provided by Sigerson Clifford, while the more recent generations are represented by John B. Keane and Brian Cleeve.

Part Two includes stories from the oral tradition. On the one hand there are pieces from storytellers whose audience would have been limited to the people of their locality, and whose art was recorded by others. Eric Cross' *The Tailor and Ansty* is a celebrated, and in its time controversial, example of this type. On the other hand we find pieces that mirror the polished and professional art of storytelling adapted for a wider public; Eamon Kelly is the obvious choice in this area.

Finally, it is hoped that these samples of the short fiction published by Mercier Press will provide the reader with the material for a very good read.

ANTHONY BLUETT

# Part One:

# The Writers

# *from* Men Withering

## Francis MacManus

'I beg your pardon,' said the stranger, in English, and moved over to make room on the seat. For a second he remained at ease, and then, rustling against the ivy, he scraped his feet nervously in the dust. 'They keep good ale here,' he said. 'Will you drink with me, sir?'

'I thank you, sir. I thank you kindly. But ale and myself ...'

'Wine, then. Let it be red wine of some kind.'

'Now, if you don't mind ...'

'Brandy? Brandy it is. Tomás! Tomás.' The tavern-keeper, soft-footed, stood in the doorway. 'A glass of brandy for this gentleman.'

'Gentleman?'

'Brandy. Put it down to me. Ah! this is the perfect place for resting.'

'You'd be a stranger to this side of the country, I'd say.'

'Yes and no! I'm travelling with some German spectacles that I'd like to part company with; but at a price, you know. At a price! But since the folk in these parts will not bid farewell with their money, I fear I must keep to my bad companions. Would you like to try a pair?'

'No! No, sir! Thank you kindly.'

'Here is the brandy for the gentleman,' said the tavern-keeper.

'They haven't any money, sir,' the old man added, sharply.

He gripped the glass that the tavern-keeper placed against his hand and after clinking against the stranger's beer-mug, he eagerly raised the liquor, sniffed and sipped. Tomás stood by and said, 'Would you like a bite before bed, Mr Hume?'

In Irish the old man broke in: 'Leave a sup of milk and a

10

bit of bread upstairs for me, will you, Tomás? I'll pay you all right. My scholar went tonight. That's a good man, Tomás.'

'Oh! I suppose I will. But mind you next week ...'

'I'll be gone Tomás. I'm going home if I can get a cart or a lift northward at all.'

'Home,' Tomás sniggered, turning away into the house.

Mr Hume drank and clapped his empty mug down on the seat. He stared at the inert figure beside him and noted how ghostly pale in the glimmer of the night was the countenance with its fringe of scant beard. A door inside the house was banged, Tomás ground out a few oaths harshly, and a dog scampered out across the yard.

'Do you make your rounds, Mr Hume,' the old man asked, ' by coach or by horseback?'

'I prefer to walk it like Adam; sometimes the stage-coach, outside of course, when I can afford it.'

'It's well to be young and travelling. Aye, indeed. I travelled a fair share of the world myself, on foot. I know every inch of this part of Munster. They know me too, but I don't know them; the people, I mean, sir. I've lived too long. More than sixty years ago I was a young man like yourself – here's to your health! – and I walked these roads and roads on the Continent, and I was in Newfoundland, too: the Land of the Fish, that is, sir, as we call it. You're a young man, aren't you?'

'Not young enough for a designing young widow, nor too old for breaking my heart on the glance of an ingenuous coquette.'

'They're fine words. Ah! but you're only a child.'

'You've seen many changes, I'm sure.'

'I have then, sir, but not so many that I wouldn't recognise the world that's in it now. It's true that once, long ago, the people daren't let on they were going to Mass of a Sunday, and school-masters like myself were no favourites of the law-men. I beg your pardon, sir, but maybe I'm offending ...'

'Not at all. I'm a Presbyterian. I'm convinced that it's a crime ...'

'A crime it is, sir. Here we are sir, paying tithes to

11

Protestant clergymen, and paying rent for holes and corners of farms, and three-quarters of us never thinking if there's a right or wrong in the matter at all. And look it, sir, there's a man up in Carrick, one of the gentry, and he's feared worse that the blackest devil out of hell. Do you know what he did one market-day? Do you know what he did? He tied two men with ropes to a cart and flogged the backs off them. Himself did, with his own hands and whip. He did.'

'You've spilled your brandy. May I call for another.'

'No, no, thank you. No, sir, thank you.' In confusion the old man muttered, sitting up stooped. The fire in him had been fire that could find little nourishment in so dry a body, and quickly he became composed and, still breathless, he began to speak again:

'For many a year of my life, sir, I hoped to die glad. What man doesn't have the hope? I hoped to see the world changing for the better and the people stirring themselves again. Maybe I don't understand things, but I'm sure the people are too far gone now. They're withered. There's little left of the old stock. Up in Dublin there's a parliament and we hear of gentlemen making speeches to poor people, poor dogs that only want to fill their bellies? Let sleeping dogs lie. They're used to the whip and the kicking boot. They won't even bark. And, mind you, sir, there was a time when they did lift a hand. I saw men fighting with sticks and stones for a few acres of grazing, but they were beaten and they lay down, and now ... ah! let the dogs lie and sleep and eat and tumble into the grave where there are no rents to be paid. All I want myself is to sit and not mind anyone.'

Casually, Hume replied, 'The French didn't lie down, I believe.'

'I heard that kind of talk. They murdered their king. They're cursed from the altars.'

'We haven't any king to murder; at least, George is not one of our own.'

'The French kept together.'

Then briskly, rising to his feet suddenly, Hume said, 'We can unite. We can, sir. We can unite.'

'We? But you're a gentleman, sir!' As he spoke, the old

12

man heard a stir in the doorway, and instantly he murmured to Hume, 'Trade in German spectacles is bad, as you say. They have no money. And besides they have good eyesight, like Tomás there at the door.'

'Oh!' Hume answered. 'Is that you, Tomás?'

'Don't be interrupting, Donnacha Mac Conmara,' Tomás rapped out in Irish. 'The gentleman was talking.'

In English Donnacha said, 'I'll be going to bed now, Mr Hume. I'm getting chilled. These old bones of mine have the winter in them for marrow. It must be near midnight anyway.'

Hume stepped up to him and placed a hand on his shoulder. 'May I help you upstairs, sir. A light, Tomás, a candle.'

Donnacha shook off the hand gently. 'I'm all right, Mr Hume. I don't need a candle. Thank you all the same. God bless your heart.'

With his left hand on the wall, he went into the house and climbed the stairway, pausing on every step to make sure of a footing on the next, and sniffing at the close air that held dead the odours of beer, damp flooring, lately baked bread and salted fish. His shuffling feet and tapping stick raised up a succession of hollow and inhospitable echoes. When he reached the room he fingered the darkness and felt with his knees the edge of the low bed. Cautiously he swept his hand across a box that served as table till he found a piece of dry bread and a cup. He began to mumble the bread with the few stumps of teeth that remained in his gums. Dry fragments trickled down his beard and coat. His ears were open to the voices from the yard.

Hume was talking, his voice full of his rigid eager energy, but only the loud gob-wide replies of Tomás mounted distinctly to the room.

'Aye! a schoolmaster, begod, without a school,' Tomás was saying. 'They say he was a poet once, but I wouldn't put much pass on what people say. Would you, sir? He just wanders around, picking up a penny here and there. He'll be getting out of this as soon as he can cadge a lift on a cart. Did you hear him about going home? He can't live much longer anyway – No sir. A bit cranky.' Then a guttural laugh. 'God bless your eyes, sir. A candle, is it? Why, Mr Hume, he's stone blind.'

He pulled up the clothes around him, and lying as straight as his stiff joints would allow him, he stroked his forehead with a thin hand.

Tomás crossed the yard, wheeled a cart over the cobbles, closed the creaking yard-gate, stood whistling softly for a minute and then, returning to the house, locked the door below with a clinking of chains. In another room, boards groaned under quietly moving feet. Presently the house was full of the sea-surge and the hiss of the unresting sycamore leaves.

*They say he was a poet once. Picking up a penny here and there.*

Instinctively he burrowed his head down among the clothes to shut out the refrain. It was queer how loss of the eyes made the ears keener and thronged the mind with echoes, tired and confused like the gab of a rabble at the end of its tether in a tavern. Damn Tomás! He would sleep. O, but he would sleep and forget. His breathing troubled him then, and he coughed out in little gasps and heard, resignedly, the wheezing of the air in the confines of old lungs. He turned over on his side and shifted the hard purse on the string from beneath his ribs.

Mouths gabbled at him out of the dark.

*Picking up a penny here and there.* Illustrem vatem parvula terra tegit. *They say he was a scholar once. A blind man can't read in the books. Blind or old, I'm a better man than the best. Good morrow, Mr Hume. Brandy for the gentleman.* Plangite, Pierides. *Don't forget me lad when you're ordained. Who will sing? Young I was and she was fair, and through the woods we went.* Plangite, plangite, plangite, plangite ...

Submissive to it all, he lay still, and all of it, even the bell-like word clanging for tears faded. *Parvula terra*, he whispered, and coughed shortly. The little pinch of clay! The dry rustle of his own whisper delayed on his hearing. He shivered.

14

The dread of mortality, the terror of the inevitable shrouding of the body, fanned him icily, till shrinking like a cat from the cold outer-world to the warmth before the fire, he wished desperately in his half-sleep for everlasting shelter against the inappeasable winds of death. He could feel them, those ceaseless winds, flowing about him, crumbling him as a desiccate lump of earth is crumbled in a heavy rainfall, pulverising him back into the dust from which he had come; and so they had been flowing, year after year, minute by minute, while the flesh bloomed healthily and then shrank to a wrinkled casing and the hair fell from the shining pate, and the bones became almost as jointless as boughs; and he, with every desire withered except the desire to live, groped and reached forward along his earthly course with an apprehensive stick. As he sank now into his half-animal sleep, his fingers twitching on the blanket, he carried with him the thought of his own decay as though it were the destiny of the people among whom he lived. He was going. So were they.

They ate, drank, slept, grew sick, bore children, quarrelled, made peace, died, and were satisfied. On the harsh weather-scarred slopes of mountains and along boggy acres, in houses and cabins built of mud against supporting ditches, in hovels that were too warm and suffocating now with the accumulated heat of the day as they would be biting cold in the brawling wintry weather, in these shelters there were men stripped of youth and old before their time, women who in hunger had borne children, and children who had begun to accept as immutable the hardship of their lives; and now they turned in sleep on the straw, or lay deadly still, or suffered wordlessly the weeping of the very young and the hungry, or listened to the cries of their beasts stabled with them on the house floors, and to the innumerable busy life in the furze thatch; or watched the faint far stars through gaps in the roof and wondered, for a moment, whether there had ever been anything else for them and their kind other than straw, mud walls, potatoes, and sleep with the beasts of the field.

Donnacha turned on his back and lay with his mouth

open. Dreams mingled. He saw what he had seen so often before he went blind: stonewalled, slated houses and mansions, some decayed with broken windows and pocked blistered woodwork, standing aloof at the ends of grassgrown avenues and drives; some kept neat, the walks gravelled and the windows curtained; and he saw himself walking the drives, going warily in dread of dogs, slipping around to an outhouse or to the kitchen-door to stand with his hat twirling in his fingers, and saying, to a servant or lackey, 'Please sir', and 'I beg of you, sir', and 'Would your honour please give a poor man a bit of bread or a scrap of meat?' Even in his sleep his hands moved to touch his forehead in obsequious salute.

He awoke, struggling to sit up.

The yard-gate was banged, resoundingly. Horses clip-clapped across the cobbles and a voice, sharp and irate, went through the house. Tomás was answering gruffly from below, growling that he was coming with a light. From the patter of footsteps, the iron shuffling of the horses and the muddle of voices, the old man picked out the jingle of spurs.

Rubbing his forehead foolishly with the palm of his hand, he settled back on the bed, and then he felt the change in the air. As sleep crept over him again, he heard dimly a door banging, footsteps pounding heavily on the stairs, then Hume's lively voice, and finally, Tomás saying: 'Some soldiers, sir. Drunk as maggots. The rest will be here tomorrow.'

Small clouds were driving in from the sea, carrying a fine and refreshing rain.

In the morning he sat on a shaft of the cart in the yard, feeling the freshness of the washed air on his face and knowing the brightness of the sun as a nebulous pale curtain only, shifting and shadowing before his dead eyes. Of the murk of the night's dreaming, there was not even a wisp in his memory. The disquieting desire to go northwards to the mountains, to his people, remained.

He was immobile, his head bent on his hands and his

hands supporting themselves on his stick, until this desire, and a sourness in his stomach turned by the old milk on which he had broken fast, gave him acute discomfort. He arose to walk, and sighed against a cramp in his meagrely fleshed thighs.

Back and forth, tapping walls and gables with his stick, he trapesed from the cart to the gateway where, on every occasion, he stood to listen. On one of these journeys, he heard the rumbling of cart-wheels, muffled in the dust. He took his stand in the middle of the road and prodded around him ostentatiously with his stick.

'Heigh! Will you get out of the way of that?' said the carter in Irish.

'Give me a hand, if you please, sir. I don't know what direction to take.'

'Walk to your left. That's it. To your left. There's the wall.'

'Would you be going north, sir? The way it is with me, I'm too stiff to do much walking. But many a time I ...'

'I'm not going north. There now, keep against the wall.'

'Would you be going north at all, sir? Wait a minute and tell me.'

'Keep back or you'll be dog's meat. I tell you I'm not going north.'

Donnacha cringed back against the wall, his back pressed against the stones, while the cart rolled past. 'You ill-mannered pup,' he said, raising his voice as the cart went farther away. 'But what do you know? When your kind were bondmen, my kin were your masters.' Instantly, he checked himself, grinned at his own poor show of temper, and returned to the yard and his seat on the cart-shaft.

'My kin were your masters,' he muttered, wondering whether his kind had ever been any better as lords than the gentry of foreign blood in the big houses. Touched by the thought as violin-strings are touched by wayward fingers, his memory released confusedly an old, half-forgotten piece of verse about the high days of the lords of Ireland, their houses and their hospitality to men of learning, clerics and poets. The verse sang up in broken lines and so he came to serenity. He was sitting thus, twining and untwining his long narrow fingers on the head of his blackthorn stick, when a voice disturbed him with 'I beg your pardon.'

It was Hume. 'I beg your pardon,' he repeated. 'Please do not stand up. Oh! please do not stand up for me. I want to apologise for any unkind word I uttered last night. It was an accident, I assure you. When I offered to find you a candle, I was not aware ...'

'That's all right, Mr Hume. I knew you were a gentleman,' Donnacha replied, almost hurt by the kindness in Hume's voice. He laughed. 'But you're a very fine gentleman to be selling spectacles!'

Hume chuckled. 'Very fine gentlemen often have sold worse wares.'

'Themselves, by heavens.' They laughed together. 'You'll not do much in the way of business in these parts,' Donnacha added. 'I mean in spectacles, sir.'

'I can try,' said Hume. 'There are some houses in the neighbourhood, and a clergyman or two.'

'Don't be talking about the French to the likes of them. If myself were listening to you long enough, you might convert me. But not them. Not in a thousand years.'

Hume was grave. 'No,' said he. 'Talking about the French is a very dangerous pastime for an honest trader.' He began to take rapid steps to and fro, always turning sharply on the ball of his foot, crunching the gravelled dust as he did so. In an undertone, he continued, 'They aren't so much afraid of the French as the example of the French.'

'They?'

'Oh! you know as well as I do. The gentry, the lords, the squires, call them what you will. They possess both the wealth and the power to make the nation prosperous and free but they use neither to that end. They fritter away their time here in the country with hunting and wenching, endless swilling of claret and rum-punch, and quarrelling like dogs about the bare bone they call honour. They had their opportunity when they were volunteers mustered in defence of their country. What did they win? Legalities, sir. What satisfies them? The gout, sir, and the pox, and half-a-dozen rapier scars from most honourable duels.' Hume snapped his fingers. 'But they know in their hearts that some day, as happened in France, they will be obliged to slaughter or be slaughtered by a people armed ...' Hume leaned against the cart and drummed his fingers on the spoke of a wheel.

'I don't understand all the English you spoke, Mr Hume. But pardon me, it sounds dangerous. What good will it do, anyway? What good did blood-swilling ever do? The country is at peace. I saw the bad days. I carry them on my back like a bag.'

'Surely,' said Hume between his teeth, 'you do not wish to have the bag, the devil's bag passed on as a legacy!'

'As long,' Donnacha replied rapidly, saying whatever came into his mind, 'as long as we have a bite and cover for the night, we're safe; we're fortunate; we're prosperous. What would the priest say to that kind of talk? Didn't the French murder and burn ... Mr Hume, speak low. Tomás, I think ...'

'Yes,' Hume murmured. 'He was in the doorway. He's gone now.'

'Don't trust him, sir. Those speeches of yours could be exchanged for King's money. And the soldiers are here!'

'So I've been told,' Hume said. 'They'll not be here tomorrow, I believe.' Then suddenly, he leaned down to the old man and whispered, 'Will you do me a favour? You see, when I make my rounds I like to have every pocket lined well with my goods. Then, with a flourish which is part of the trade I can pull out spectacles for every manner of complaint. Now, I happen to have a packet of private letters which I hold very dear. They're quite private, I swear to you. They take up much room in my pocket. I should be obliged to you if you would take charge of them till I return tonight or perhaps, in the morning. I'd rather not leave them in my room. Tomás pries too much. Besides, these soldiers are no respecters of the property they are paid to protect. Do I ask too ...?'

'You're asking nothing, sir. Nothing at all. They're safe with me. I can't read them anyway.'

Hume pressed closer to Donnacha and thrust a bulky

19

packet into the left-hand pocket of his coat. Then, into one of the palms resting on the knob of a blackthorn stick he pressed a coin. The thin fingers closed greedily. 'A sovereign, sir?' said Donnacha. 'A whole sovereign?' He coughed for a breath with excitement. 'I can go miles. I can go miles now.'

'Drink my health today and tomorrow,' Hume said quietly. 'And may I ask for one more favour. If you do not mind, please say a prayer for me.' Then, Hume, with quick decisive steps was gone.

A hush, like the silence left after an army has marched by in haste, possessed the yard.

Involuntarily, Donnacha Ruadh pulled himself to his feet and turned his head from side to side. A vague alarm of oncoming menace moved him. All he remembered of the man who walked down the road, was an orderly strong assault of words and he tried to fix his mind on them. There was new hope in them, he surmised, as heartening and yet as frightening as a wandering light far-out in a bog is to a lost man. But what was it? What in the name of God was the sense of it? He relaxed to his seat on the shaft. The old broken verse about the lords of Ireland in their hey-day, welled up and drowned all questioning with slow regret and black lamentation for the dead.

# The Black Chafer

## Padraic Pearse*

It was a tramp from the Joyce country who came into our house one wild wintry night that told us the story of the 'Black Chafer' as we sat around the fire.

The wind was wailing around the house, like women keening the dead, as he was speaking, and he made his voice rise or fall according as the wind rose or fell.

He was a tall man with wild eyes and his clothes were almost in tatters. In a way, I was afraid of him, when I first saw him, and his story did nothing to lessen that fear.

'The three most blessed animals in the world,' he said, 'are the haddock, the robin and the lady-bird. And the three most cursed animals are the snake, the wren and the black chafer. And the black chafer is the most cursed of them all.

'I know that only too well. If a man should kill your son, woman of the house, never call him a black chafer, or if a woman should come between you and your husband, don't compare her with the black chafer.'

'God save us,' my mother said.

'Amen,' he replied.

The tramp didn't speak again for some time. We all stayed quiet because we knew he was going to tell us a story. It wasn't long before he began.

When I was a boy (he began), there was a woman in our village that everyone was afraid of. She lived in a little lonely cabin in a mountain-gap and nobody would ever go near her house. Neither would she come near anyone's house herself. Nobody would speak to her when they met her on the road, and she never stopped to talk with anybody either.

You would have pity for the creature just to see her walking the roads by herself, alone.

---

* From *Short Stories of Padraic Pearse* selected and adapted by Desmond Maguire.

'Who is she,' I used to ask my mother, 'or why won't they speak to her?'

'Shh-hh-boy,' she always replied. 'That's the Black Chafer, a woman with a curse on her.'

'What did she do or who put the curse on her?'

'She was cursed by a priest, they say, but nobody knows what she did.'

And that's all the information I could get about her until I was a grown chap. Even then, I could find out nothing, except that she committed some dreadful sin, when she was young, and that she was cursed publicly by a priest on account of it. One Sunday, when the people were assembled at Mass, the priest turned around and said from the altar:

'There is a woman here that will merit eternal damnation for herself and for every person friendly with her. And I say to that woman, that she is a cursed woman, and I say to you, to be as neighbourly to her, as you would be to a black chafer.'

Then he said: 'Rise up now, Black Chafer, and avoid the company of decent people from this out!'

The poor woman got up and went out of the chapel. She was never called anything after that, except The Black Chafer, and her real name was soon forgotten. It was said that she had the evil eye. If she ever looked on a calf or sheep that wasn't her own, the animals died. Before long, the women were afraid to let their children out on the village-street if she was passing by.

I married a very attractive girl when I was twenty-one. We had a little girl and were expecting another child. One day when I was cutting turf on the bog, my wife was feeding the hens in the street, when she saw – God between us and harm – the Black Chafer coming up the bohereen carrying the girl in her arms. One of the child's arms was woven around the woman's neck, and her shawl covered the mite's little body. My wife was speechless!

The Black Chafer laid the little girl in her mother's arms and my wife noticed that her clothes were wet.

'What happened the child?' she asked.

'She was looking for water-lilies around the Pool of the

Rushes when she fell in,' the woman replied. 'I was crossing the road when I heard her screaming. I jumped over the ditch and managed to catch her just in the nick of time.'

'May God reward you,' said my wife. The other woman went off before she had time to say anymore. My wife brought the child inside, dried her and put her to bed. When I came home from the bog she told me what had happened. We both prayed for the Black Chafer that night.

The following day, the little girl began to prattle about the woman that saved her. 'The water was in my mouth, and in my eyes and in my ears,' she told us, 'I saw shining sparks and heard a great noise; I was slipping and slipping and suddenly I felt a hand about me, and she lifted me up and kissed me. I thought I was at home when I was in her arms with her shawl around me.'

A few days after that, my wife discovered that the child was missing. She was missing for a couple of hours. When she came home, she told us that she was after paying a visit to the woman that saved her life. 'She made a cake for me,' she told us. 'There is nobody in the house but herself so I promised her that I'd call in to see her every day.'

Neither my wife nor I could say a word against her. The Black Chafer was after saving the girl's life so it wouldn't have been natural to prevent her from going up to the lonely house in the gap of the mountain. From that day onwards the child went up the hill to see her every evening.

The neighbours told us that it wasn't right. In a way, we knew that we were wrong, but how could we help it?

Would you believe me, friends? From the day the Black Chafer laid eyes on the little girl she began to dwindle and dwindle like a fire that couldn't be kindled! She soon lost her appetite and strength and after three months she was only a shadow. A month later she was in the churchyard.

The Black Chafer came down the mountain the day she was buried. They wouldn't let her into the graveyard. She turned back sorrowfully and slowly traced her footsteps up the mountain path again. I pitied the poor creature, because I knew that our trouble was no heavier than her own.

The next morning I went up the mountain path myself. I

meant to tell her that neither my wife nor myself bore her any grudge or blamed her for what had happened. I knocked at her door but got no answer. I went in and saw that the ashes were red on the hearth. There was nobody at all to be seen. Then I noticed a bed in a corner of the room, so I went over to it. The Black Chafer was lying on it ... cold and dead.

From that day onwards my household and myself have been plagued with disaster. My wife died in childbirth a month afterwards. The baby didn't survive. My cattle picked up some disease the following winter and the landlord put me out of my holding. I have been travelling the roads of Connacht, as a walking man, ever since.

# The White Goat

## Seamus O'Kelly*

The white goat stood in a little clearing closed in by a ring of whins on the hillside. Her head swayed from side to side like the slow motion of the pendulum of a great clock. The legs were a little spread, the knees bent, the sides slack, the snout grey and dry, the udder limp.

The Herd knew the white goat was in great agony. She had refused the share of bran he had brought her, had turned away from the armful of fresh ivy leaves his little daughter held out to her. He had desisted from the milking, she had moaned so continuously.

Some days before the Herd had found the animal injured on the hill; the previous night he had heard the labourers making a noise, shouting and singing, as they crossed from the tillage fields. He knew what had happened when he had seen the marks of their hobnailed boots on her body. She was always a sensitive brute, of a breed that came from the lowlands. The sombre eyes of the Herd glowed in a smouldering passion as he stood helplessly by while the white goat swung her head from side to side.

He gathered some dry bracken and spread a bed of it near the white goat. It would be unkind to allow her to lie on the wet grass when the time came that she could no longer stand. He looked up at the sky and marked the direction of the wind. It had gone round to the west. Clouds were beginning to move across the sky. There was a vivid light behind the mountains. The air was still. It would rain in the night. He had thought for the white goat standing there in the darkness, swaying her head in agony, the bracken growing sodden at her feet, the rain beating into her eyes. It was a cold place and wind-swept. Whenever the white goat had broken her tether she had flown from it to the lowlands. He

---

* From *Irish Short Stories* by Seamus O'Kelly.

remembered how, while leading her across a field once, she had drawn back in some terror when they had come to a pool of water.

The Herd looked at his little daughter. The child had drawn some distance away, the ivy leaves fallen from her bare arms. He was conscious that some fear had made her eyes round and bright. What was it that the child feared? He guessed, and marvelled that a child should understand the strange thing that was about to happen up there on the hill. The knowledge of Death was shining instinctively in the child's eyes. She was part of the stillness and greyness that was creeping over the hillside.

'We will take the white goat to the shelter of the stable,' the Herd said.

The child nodded, the fear still lingering in her eyes. He untied the tether and laid his hand on the horn of the goat. She answered to the touch, walking patiently but unsteadily beside him.

After a while the child followed, taking the other horn, gently, like her father, for she had all his understanding of and nearness to the dumb animals of the fields. They came slowly and silently. The light failed rapidly as they came down the hill. Everything was merged in a shadowy vagueness, the colour of the white goat between the two dim figures alone proclaiming itself. A kid bleated somewhere in the distance. It was the cry of a young thing for its suckle, and the Herd saw that for a moment the white goat raised her head, the instinct of her nature moving her. Then she tottered down the hill in the darkness.

When they reached the front of the stable the white goat backed painfully from the place. The Herd was puzzled for a moment. Then he saw the little pool of water in a faint glimmer before their feet. He brought the animal to one side, avoiding it, and she followed the pressure of his directing hand.

He took down a lantern that swung from the rafters of the stable and lighted it. In a corner he made a bed of fresh straw. The animal leaned over a little against the wall, and they knew she was grateful for the shelter and the support.

Then the head began to sway in a weary rhythm from side to side as if the pain drove it on. Her breath quickened, broke into little pants. He noted the thin vapour that steamed from about her body. The Herd laid his hand on her snout. It was dry and red hot. He turned away, leading the child by the hand, the lantern swinging from the other, throwing long yellow streaks of light about the gloom of the stable. He closed the door softly behind him.

It was late that night when the Herd got back from his rounds of the pastures. His boots soaked in the wet ground and the clothes clung to his limbs, for the rain had come down heavily. A rumble of thunder sounded over the hills as he raised the latch of his door. He felt glad he had not left the white goat tethered in the whins on the hill.

His little daughter had gone to sleep. His wife told him the child on being put to bed had wept bitterly, but refused to confess the cause of her grief. The Herd said nothing, but he knew the child had wept for the white goat. The thought of the child's emotion moved him, and he turned out of the house again, standing in the darkness and the rain. Why had they attacked the poor brute? He asked the question over and over again, but only the rain beat in his face and around him was darkness, mystery. Then he heard the voices higher up on the side of the hill, first for a laugh, then some shouts and cries. A thick voice raised the refrain of a song, and it came booming through the murky atmosphere. The Herd could hear the words:

Where are the legs with which you run?
Hurroo! Hurroo!
Where are the legs with which you run
When first you went to carry a gun?
Indeed your dancing days are done!
Och, Johnny, I hardly knew ye!

And then came the chorus like a roar down the hills:

With drums and guns, and guns and drums
The enemy nearly slew ye!
My darling dear, you look so queer,

27

Och, Johnny, I hardly knew ye!

The voices of the labourers passing from the tillage fields died away, and the rumble of thunder came down more frequently from the hills. The Herd crossed his garden, his boots sinking in the soft ground. Half way across he paused, for a loud cry had dominated the fury of the breaking storm. His ears were quick for the cries of animals in distress. He went on rapidly toward the stable.

The ground grew more sloppy and a thin stream of water came from the rim of his face. He noted the flashes of lightning overhead. Through it all the cry of the white goat sounded, with that weird, vibrating 'mag-gag' that was the traditional note of her race. It had a powerful appeal for the Herd. It stirred a feeling of passion within him as he hurried through the rain.

How they must have lacerated her, a poor brute chained to the sod, at the mercy of their abuse! The red row of marks along her gams, raw and terrible, sprang to his sight out of the darkness. Vengeance, vengeance! He gripped his powerful hands, opening and closing fists. Then he was conscious of something in the storm and the darkness, that robbed him of his craving for personal vengeance. All that belonged to the primitive man welled up in him. He knew that in the heart of the future there lurked a reckoning – something, somebody – that would count the tally at the appointed time. Then he had turned round the gable of the stable. He saw the ghostly white thing, shadowy in the blackness, lying prostrate before the door. He stood still, his breath drawn inward.

There was a movement in the white shape. He could discern the blurred outline of the head of the animal as she raised it up a little. There was a low moan followed by a great cry. The Herd stood still, terror in his heart. For he interpreted that cry in all the terrible inarticulate consciousness of his own being. That cry sounded in his ears like an appeal to all the generations of wronged dumb things that had ever come under the lash of this tyranny of men. It was the protest of the brute creation against humanity, and to the

Herd it was a judgment. Then his eyes caught a murky gleam beside the fallen white shape, and the physical sense of things jumped back to his mind.

He remembered that in wet weather a pool of water always gathered before the stable door. He remembered that there was a glimmer of it there when he had led the white goat into the stable. He remembered how she had shown fear of it.

He stooped down over the white goat where she lay. Thin wisps of her hair floated about looking like dim wraiths against the blackness of the pool. He caught a look of the brown eyes and was aware that the udder and teats bulged up from the water. He sank down beside her, the water making a splash as his knees dropped into the place. The animal raised her head a little and with pain, for the horns seemed to weigh like lead. But it was an acknowledgment that she was conscious of his presence; then the head fell back, a gurgle sounding over one of the ears.

The Herd knew what had happened, and it was all very tragical to his mind. His wife had come out to the stable for something, and had left the door open behind her. The white goat, goaded by the growing pain, had staggered out the door, perhaps feeling some desire for the open fields in her agony. Then she had seen before the threshold of the door that which had always been a horror to her – a pool of water. The Herd could see her tottering and swaying and then falling into it with a cry, fulfilling her destiny. He wondered if he himself had the same instinct for the things that would prove fatal to him? Why was he always so nervous when he stooped to or lay upon the ground? Why did it always give him a feeling that he would be trampled under the hooves of stampeding cattle rounded up for treatment for the warble fly? He trembled as he heard the beat of hooves on the ground behind him. He peered about and for a while did not recognise the shape that moved restlessly about in the darkness. He heard the neigh of the brood mare. He knew then she had been hovering about the stable afraid to go in out of the storm. She was afraid to go in because of the thing that lay before the stable door. He heard the answering call of the young foal in the stable, and he knew that it, too, was afraid to come out even at the call of its dam. Death was about in that night of storm, and all things seemed conscious of it.

He stooped down over the white goat and worked his hands under her shoulders. He lifted her up and felt the strain all over his frame, the muscles springing tense on his arms. She was a dead weight, and he had always prided on her size. His knees dug into the puddle in the bottom of the pool as he felt the pressure of his haunches. He strained hard as he got one of his feet under him. With a quick effort he got the other foot into position and rose slowly, lifting the white form out of the pool. The shaggy hair hung from the white goat, limp and reeking, numerous thin streams of water making a little ripple as they fell. The limbs of the Herd quivered under the weight, he staggered back, his heavy boots grinding in the gravel; then he set his teeth, the limbs steadied themselves, he swayed uncertainly for a moment, then staggered across the stable door, conscious of the hammer strokes of the heart of the white goat beating against his own heart. He laid her down in the bed of straw and heard the young foal bounding out of the stable in terror. The Herd stood in the place, the sweat breaking out on his forehead, then dropping in great beads.

The white goat began to moan. The Herd was aware from the rustling of the straw that her limbs were working convulsively. He knew from the nature of her wounds that her death would be prolonged, her agonies extreme. What if he put her out of pain? It would be all over in a moment. His hand went to his pocket, feeling it on the outside. He made out the shape of the knife, but hesitated.

One of the hooves of the white goat struck him on the ankle as her limbs worked convulsively. His hand went into his pocket and closed around the weapon. He would need to be quick and sure, to have a steady hand, to make a swift movement. He allowed himself some moments to decide. Then the blade of the knife shot back with a snap.

The sound seemed to reach the white goat in all its grim significance. She struggled to her feet, moaning more loudly.

30

The Herd began to breathe hard. He was afraid she would cry out even as she had cried out as she lay in the pool before the stable door. The terror of the things that made up that cry broke in upon the Herd. He shook with fear of it. Then he stooped swiftly, his fingers nervously feeling over the delicate course of the throat of the white goat. His hands moved a little backwards and forwards in the darkness. He felt the hot stream on his hands, then the animal fell without a sound, her horns striking against the wall. He stood over for a moment and was conscious that his hands were wet. Then he remembered with a shudder that the whole tragedy of the night had been one of rains and pools and water and clinging damp things, of puddles and sweats and blood. Even now the knife he held in his fingers was dripping. He let it fall. It fell with a queer thud, sounding of flesh, of a dead body. It had fallen on the dead body of the white goat. He turned with a groan and made his way uncertainly for the stable door.

At the door he stood, thoughts crowding in upon, questions beating upon his brain and giving no time for answer. Around him was darkness, mystery, Death. What right had he to thrust his hand blindly into the heart of this mystery? Who had given him the power to hasten the end, to summon Death before its time? Had not Nature her own way for counting out the hours and the minutes? Had not she, or some other power, appointed an hour for the white goat to die? She would live, even in agony, until they could bear her up no longer; and having died Nature would pass her through whatever channel her laws had ordained. Had not the white goat made her last protest against his interference when she had risen to her feet in her death agony? And if the white goat, dumb beast that she was, had suffered wrong at the hands of man, then there was, the Herd now knew, a Power deliberate and inexorable, scrupulous in its delicate adjustment of right and wrong, that would balance the account at the appointed audit.

He had an inarticulate understanding of these things as he moved from the stable door. He tripped over a barrow unseen in the darkness and fell forward on his face into the field. As he lay there he heard the thudding of hooves on the ground. He rose dizzy and unnerved, to see the dim shapes of some cattle that had gathered down about the place from the upland. He felt the rain beating upon his face, the clothes hung dank and clammy to his limbs. His boots soaked and slopped when he stepped. A boom of thunder sounded overhead and a vivid flash of lightning lit up for an instant a great elm tree. He saw all its branches shining with water, drops glistening along a thousand stray twigs. Then the voices of the labourers returning over the hills broke in upon his ears. He heard their shouts, the snatches of their songs, their noise, all the ribaldry of men merry in their drink.

The Herd groped through the darkness for his house like a half-blind man, his arms out before him and a sudden gust of wind that swept the hillside shrieked about the blood of the white goat that was still wet upon his hands.

# The Return

## Daniel Corkery[*]

Where Ankle Lane joins Blarney Street there are four high houses, dark-looking and very old, of that sort lane-dwellers call 'fabrics' or 'castles'. The number of inhabitants varies from day to day: tricky-men in for the races will stay two nights, cattle-drovers only one; in periods of idleness a group of coal-porters sometimes attains a certain solidarity – the same figures go in and out the doors day after day – but, just as happens in a factory, change sets in with prosperity; new faces come and go; and the next period of idleness sees a new colony, the same in its general characteristics, though made up of quite different individuals, repeat the fortunes of the last.

The largest, the darkest of these four houses was kept by a widow named Tynan; Bonnety Tynan she was called from a wisp of a bonnet that clung to her scanty hairs; the other lodging-house keepers wore shawls. Her face was crabbed, shut like a fist against craft, reduced to its smallest and toughest by dint of years of hard-dealing. And her bonnet was equally shorn of its beams; this, too, was now not much bigger than a fist, but the legend still held that it was the lodging-house keeper's money-box. Sometimes she would have as many as thirty men under her roof, most of them idle, so her hardness, her aloofness were needed. How else could she have managed them? The Law? – it was too complicated; and besides, she kept too irregular a house to care to invoke it. She had laws and ejectment-processes of her own. Sometimes she conceived suspicion of a lodger; she waited till his back was turned; then she would slap a few buckets of water over his bed; he returned to find it sodden; and she went on with her washing while he stamped and

---

[*] From *A Munster Twilight* by Daniel Corkery.

---

cursed.

In the beginning of winter, one evening towards six o'clock, as she shuffled in along the dark hall, she was surprised to see a glare of firelight breaking out towards her from the kitchen; she had been out of the house for some hours and hoped for nothing better than a spark in the bottom of the grate.

Opening the squeaking door she was still more surprised; a great figure, a darkness, sat on a stool before the fire; she noticed the curving width of his back; the huge head bent forward – he was asleep. She went silently up to him, bending to see his face; it was tanned; she glanced at his hands; they were dark with tar, knobbly, and had blue rings and flags tattooed on them; but it was the hard, exaggerated-looking creases in his serge clothes that spoke his trade most clearly – these clothes had been folded tightly for weeks, perhaps for months, in the bottom of a seaman's chest. She shook him: 'Come on now – wake up, who are 'oo? who are 'oo?'

He growled; then his voice softened; he rose and stretched himself, very much at his ease; a light came into his sea-bleared eyes; he examined the old woman's face with interest, with amusement apparently. 'You're not changed a ha'p'oth,' he said, 'not a ha'p'orth.'

'Sit down,' she said, 'I can't call to mind what your name is – 'tis after escaping me mimory.'

With a seaman's licence he put his great arm about her, drew her towards the glowing fire, and said again:

'You're not changed a ha'p'oth.'

'I don't know you,' she snapped out, breaking away.

'If you don't there's not a soul in Cork to say who I am – I'm Jim Daunt that was.'

A memory or two, quite unimportant, stirred in her brain: 'So you are, so you are; you're welcome; how long will you be staying?'

'Till half-past eleven anyway,' he said.

'Where's the boat – Queenstown?'

'No – the jetties,' he answered, 'and I must be aboard for midnight.'

She treated him well; she gave him a couple of eggs and many rounds of bread; yet for a seaman he made but a scanty meal.

'You're not doing well?' she said.

'If I only had it yesterday,' he said, 'you'd see the death I'd give it.'

She moved about in the silent way of a woman who is accustomed to keep people at a distance. It was he who spoke:

'Isn't this a quare thing,' he said, 'I was never a bit lonesome wherever I was on sea or land – thousands of miles away – never a bit lonesome till this evening sitting there on that there stool?'

She believed him; for she knew these sailormen well; and how any shelter that has the look, or even the name of home, stirs them.

'You were a great long time out,' he continued, half-complaining.

'How did I know you'd be here?'

'When did you leave the house?'

'Near four, I expect.'

'Well, now, look at that,' he said. 'You mustn't have been well round the corner when I came in; and here I stopped, for I couldn't go away again – couldn't go away. Was I asleep when you came in?'

A lodger they called Brother entered; Mrs Tynan made the two men known to each other. The sailorman wanted drink to be sent for; Bonnety however wouldn't have it; there was plenty of time, and besides, drink was no food for a man after a day's work. Brother seconded her; Saturday Night would be coming in soon, and he was the best of company; it was company a man wanted after being shut up for months in a wind-bag. 'Wasn't it, matey?' he said, taking the seaman's hand. A radiance had come into Brother's face: unexpected joy is straight from the hands of the gods: exhausted, heavy in all his limbs from climbing with a laden hod forty-foot ladders from early morning – terrible work – he had hoped for nothing beyond a single drink in Miss Nora's, and lo! the pleasures of a revel were emerging in his imagination.

'Have you enough of it?' he said.

'Of what?'

'The say.'

'God knows an' I have,' said the sailor, with unexpected earnestness, 'but isn't it a quare thing to say that I was never a bit lonesome till this evening sitting there on that there stool?'

'How so?' said Brother.

And then with lingering detail the sailor told how he had kept watch while Mrs Tynan was down in Miss Nora's.

Saturday Night came in after a few moments; in every feature, in every limb he had become misshapen by dint of combat; his most restful attitude challenged; yet in Brother's words he was the best of company; spirit is spirit.

Brother, introducing the men, mentioned the sailor's former connection with the house; 'There's no house like the old house,' he said, and Saturday Night, gripping the sailor's hand, told him that though he had never met him before, he felt they were old friends already; 'There's something draws me to you,' he said, and the sailor answered; 'A fellow don't hear words like them from foreigners.'

And three minutes afterwards he told Saturday Night that he had never known what it was to be down-hearted till that evening, sitting on that there stool before the fire. And, indicating Brother, 'Himself will tell you,' he answered Saturday Night's look of inquiry.

Again he wanted to send out for drink; but again the landlady blanked the proposal: 'What hurry was there? wasn't the night long enough? couldn't they wait for Johnny Swaine at least?'

Instead of Johnny Swaine came Katty Sullivan, saying as her first word:

'Isn't Johnny here?'

'Not yet,' and they bade her sit down.

'By James, I might as well,' she said: the form of swear she had invented herself, and its use seemed to lift her above the common throng; yet she needed no such aid; by nature she was above her surroundings. Strong and happy, with full, firm flesh, her face coloured like ripe corn, her eyes blue and bright as the skies that go with it, she was large-hearted, and merry and frank because of her fearlessness, of her consciousness of power.

'Here's a lonely sailorman, wouldn't object to a bit of company,' said Saturday Night, 'and 'tis a thing no wan objects to,' she answered, in a tone that had as much daring as pity in it. Her words seemed to take the sailorman off his guard; the impudence in his face withered before her eyes. She had laid her spell on him; but everyone saw that some weakness of spirit denied his rising to it: he looked like a sick sportsman who on a morning of sunshine suddenly discovers that he is unable to lift his body from the bed. The moment's unrest was swallowed in a whirl of words, for Katty Sullivan was one they all liked to talk with. She was one of those who, though they might give a man a 'wipe' across the mouth, never get on their dignity, an attitude that takes all heart out of a night's merriment. Soon Johnny Swaine came seeking Katty, even as she had been seeking him; and the sailor saw at once that he was her accepted lover, and with the knowledge a touch of daring came back into his look; his eyes, in spite of himself as it were, would now find themselves resting on Johnny's face. Brother was sent for drink; he returned with two friends; "twould go to me heart to refuse them,' he explained to the sailor.

The sailor drank nothing but raw whiskey, and it soon appeared that his loneliness had gone from him; so too had his hold on himself. He became aggressive; when Brother was telling his champion tale of a sailor who, having deserted, signed on again in the self-same ship under stress of drink, the sailor stopped him half-way, and in his mouth the story from being a mere fill-gap became wild and thrilling. And almost without a pause he went on to tell the story of a parson's daughter of Adelaide, the girl who hid herself in the ship's hold for the sake of the young captain – how she might now be met with in the cities of the South American seaboard, in Buenos Aires or Rio – the sailors speak of her as the Australian Rose. He had seen her himself. His voice became higher and louder; he seemed to be talking against time, and his eyes shifted continually from face to face. He twitted Brother on his powers of drinking; he joked Saturday Night on his wounds; yet somehow his merriment was not contagious; and they all sniffed trouble when he began to raise bad blood between the lovers, for they could see that Katty's eyes were rife for mischief.

Johnny she said would have gone sailoring himself only for the wetness of the sea and his love for his mother; anyway, he wouldn't like to be pickled as well as drowned and, by James! she wouldn't care to see him pickled herself; 'he'd be a terrible sight!' Then the sailor, with great concern, asked her what would she do if Johnny went off with another girl? She laughed, bent with laughter at the idea, and the whole room laughed uneasily with her. And so Johnny Swaine, made scapegoat for the company, sat by the girl's side, looking with glum eyes at his unfinished drink. But when at the end of a bout of merriment the sailor stretched his hand to him saying that a joke was a joke, Johnny would not even look at the proffered hand. 'Anyway, fetch us the measure,' the sailor continued with some diplomacy; and Swaine, thinking of peace with honour, rose from his place and made for the can. Without a sound the sailor sprang into the vacant space at the girl's side, and Johnny, turning, found him there. A roar of laughter addled him, maddened him. He flung the gallon about the floor, squared out, and his voice rose above the jubilee: 'Stand up, if you're a man.'

'Miss Sullivan,' the sailor's voice was heard saying in the sudden, expectant silence, 'isn't it lovely weather?'

'Stand up, I say.'

'A beautiful night?'

'Will you stand up?'

And the girl's eyes danced to see such spirit in her lover.

'You won't, won't you?' and Johnny's open hand met the sailor's cheek with a ringing blow. In a flash the two men were dancing at each other, the sailor all activity, his voice jerking out the best known of all the chanties:

Ranzo was no sailor;

Ranzo, boys, Ranzo.

And every time he came to 'Ranzo' in the refrain – the word
on which the rope is dragged as they hoist sail – he struck or
rather touched Johnny's face or side or ears: he played with
the landsman, dancing round him, tipping him wherever he
wished.

> The captain was a bad man;
> Ranzo, boys, Ranzo!
> The mate he was a good man;
> Ranzo, boys, Ranzo!

The company seeing that he did not mean to punish his man
let their mirth loose; they began to cry out: 'Go it, Johnny, go
it, old man.' But after some time the sailor became over-
confident, became careless; Johnny, on the other hand, had
recovered his self-possession. Seeing a chance, he stood
statue-still for a moment; then, making a wild charge, struck
full in the sailor's face. The sea-blood fired up; song and
dance ceased; with swift, careful drives he drove Johnny
back, back, almost into the fire-grate. The room had become
silent. Both men seemed to be fighting for life. They panted;
their feet scraped the floor. Katty stood up: 'Sir', she said, in
a breathy voice that was scarcely audible, 'Sir, sir', but
neither fighters nor onlookers heard her at all.

Suddenly shuffling steps were heard coming in the hall,
and 'Police', whispered Brother; for policeman walk into
such houses in the same manner as factory-inspectors walk
into factories. At the word the sailor's face went white; he
turned half-round from his man towards the room door; and
Johnny, who had not perhaps heard Brother's warning,
battered him right and left with great will.

'Wait awhile,' said the sailor, all confusion, still staring
at the door.

'Come on,' shouted Johnny, wondering what had happened.

All faces were on the door; some of the men were gripping others by the shoulders. It was old Ned Mulcahy, the
mason, who stuck in his head. The next moment the sailor

was dancing once more around Johnnny.

He gave him five and twenty;
Ranzo, boys, Ranzo.

His terror had lifted; he resumed his antics, and soon he had Johnny jammed into a corner, where he kept him until he had his nose pumping blood. Then the combatants were separated.

'He's a game fighter anyway,' said the sailor, releasing him; and Katty Sullivan, passing the defeated man a handkerchief, thought in her heart of hearts that she wouldn't give him for all the tanned-faced sailors on the sea.

It was now high time for the sailor to be going if he was to make his ship by midnight; yet he dawdled to hear the end of a story, to turn a joke, to look at Johnny's nose. He lingered too long; for Saturday Night suddenly began to tell the tale he always reserved till he had become quite emotional in his drink. They were unloading the *Cyclamen* he said, and the first glimmer of dawn was coming on the river and, merciful God! he saw a woman floating down the tide, her golden hair spread out on top of the water. They got her into a boat – the handsomest woman he ever laid eyes on, and he tried to persuade the men to say nothing at all about the matter, only just take the corpse up to Burnt Lane on a shutter and give her a decent wake with candles, and Christian burial in the Gardens; but they wouldn't, they were afraid of the law; and the police came, and the first words the sergeant said were (and Saturday Night wept to repeat them): 'What do you know about this *person*?' 'What do you know about this *person*?' Saturday Night spoke the words again, turning towards the sailor; and 'Was that what he said?' the sailor gasped out, but his voice was so strange that the whole room on the instant forgot the story; the sailor's jaw had become locked, his neck rigid, his head looked as if carved in hardwood, the eyes unskilfully painted – a blank stare. But he lifted himself up, and 'I'll be late,' he said, in a voice that beseeched them not to question or hinder him; he had broken down; he could not explain himself – at least, this is what they would think.

'Good night,' he said, putting out his hand to Katty Sullivan in a sudden, jerky way, his eyes meanwhile turned away from all the faces. She took no notice; she let on to be speaking to Johnny, who was now once more at her side. Without another word the sailor vanished from their midst.

After a pause the old woman spoke in her hardest voice: 'Did any of ye see that fellow coming in here?'

No one spoke; in the silence Brother cracked a match on the bowl of his pipe.

'He said he came in here today after I wint out.'

'And sure he might.'

'I'd like to know,' the old woman rejoined, and she lit two candles – a signal for them to retire.

'He said he was asleep,' she added, 'he was no more asleep than I was.'

'Holy Mother!' said Katty Sullivan, as she rose to go, 'I'm sorry I iver laid eyes on him.'

Now, I think that the sailor, as he stumbled down the deserted hillside streets towards the river, shook himself and stood still a moment here, stood still a moment elsewhere, saying at every pause; ''Twill be all right – what a fool I am!'

Anyway, he got to his ship; made to walk up the plank with his head in the air, and – who knows how the end came?

But the next day they brought up two dead bodies from between his ship and the quay-wall; one of them, the second mate it was, had a knife-wound in the right lung and another in the back below the lung; the second body, bearing no signs of struggle on it, was our sailorman, Jim Daunt; and it was proved by the stopping of their watches and other- wise that one body had been a couple of hours longer in the water than the other. Saturday Night says that as he went up the plank maybe he heard a voice saying 'What do you know about this *person*?' but Brother says that 'tis how he threw himself in, for he saw that the whole race of men were turning against him – look at how Katty Sullivan, with no reason at all, *couldn't* shake hands with him. Johnny Swaine

41

says they all came well out of it, as if a murderer has evil spirits at his beck and call.

But what brought the sailorman up to Bonnety Tynan's at all? Was he trying to prove an alibi? Or was it that the word Home had been for years ringing in his brain?

# The Awakening

## Pádraic Ó Conaire[*]

I was so road-weary that I decided to sleep until midday, in order to refresh myself. I had not lain on a bed for a month previously, and I was at first rather loath to lie between the cold white sheets. It was the kind of feeling one has before taking the first plunge into the sea on the coming of summer. Going to bed was such a novel sensation that I almost made up my mind not to undress! What a cold, forbidding appearance these white sheets presented! I began to shiver before I jumped in.

But once in, I was at ease. I stretched and again drew in my limbs. I looped myself like an eel. I turned on my right side; then on my left; and then, as if wishing not to lose any of the comfort of the bed, I lay on my back. I drew a long, easy breath – like one who had feasted with royalty. Then I gazed upwards at the ceiling, round at the white walls and across at the two tightly closed windows. I thought I had never slept in a more pleasant place.

Who would sleep in a forest glade or on a lake shore or beside a murmuring brook, however sheltered the places might be, while such shelter as I now enjoyed was to be found nearby in a mountain hut! It is all very well for the poets to sing of dark gloomy forests, of foggy glens, of bright rivers, of starry dark-blue skies, of the golden sunset, of the blackbird warbling in the early morning; but as for me I vowed I would forsake them all henceforth, and would sleep only between white sheets in a small airtight room, having a white ceiling over me, and white walls around me.

How delightful it was to have an opportunity of shaking off my weariness in such surroundings. Is there any other comfort comparable with it? Do not mention to me the joys

---

[*] From *Field and Fair* by Pádraic Ó Conaire, translated by Cormac Breathnach.

of heaven! everybody has his heaven in his own heart, and the heaven of one may not be the heaven of another. But he who cannot enjoy a fine feather bed with white sheets and pillow and bolster must be a bad cantankerous fellow. Place no confidence in him; don't cultivate his friendship or his society. He is not a man of his word ...

Beware of the man who prefers starry dark-blue heavens to a pretty ceiling over him, who prefers to lie on the ground underneath a fragrant flowery briar than between two sheets – beware of him. He may be a poet, but nevertheless be on your guard; he will abandon you in your hour of need. That, at all events, was my thought as I lay for the first time in a month between the sheets in my little white room.

I lit my pipe and sent upwards a cloud of beautiful blue smoke, and that smoke assumed more pleasing shapes than ever I beheld on heavenly clouds at the hour of sunrise. I spent a considerable time watching these smoke clouds that wafted so airily above me.

How pleasantly heated my limbs became! Henceforth let no one dilate to me on the heat that comes from the sun as one reclines on a mossy bank in the forenoon, nor on the heat given out by a good fire on a cold night when the earth is frost-bound; mention them not because they are not worth mentioning when compared with the sensation of heat one who has slept for a long time under the canopy of heaven feels in his bones and limbs when lying between two sheets. There is no heat, no pleasure, no bodily comfort to equal that ...

Did you ever notice an infant three months old lying nude before a fire! Did you observe how quiet, how satisfied it looks? It stretches its little soft limbs, draws them up, while all the time its half-shut eyes are glistening with joy.

It gives expression to its delight by ejaculating gloo-oo-oo, and by twisting and turning its little body. I felt the joy of that babe as I was shaking off my woe and weariness between the clean white sheets.

And if I didn't make a ball of myself as the naked baby does before the fire, the flesh, not the spirit was at fault.

I became absorbed in thought. Strange fleeting fancies

came into my mind; and no sooner would one take posses-
sion than it would be ousted by another. They came separ-
ately and in groups – stray thoughts that have been since the
beginning of time wandering round the world seeking in
vain a place in which to take root and grow and increase
until they lit on this miserable person lying between unac-
customed sheets.

I struggled valiantly against them. I endeavoured to
catch one of them and squeeze the blood and marrow out of
it, but it eluded me. I had as little chance of catching a
sunbeam.

But no sooner would one be gone than a worse would
take its place. I resolved to pay no heed to them, good, bad
or indifferent; then they became ever so much bolder and
more daring. They were like a host of mocking devils teasing
and tormenting me. The day was breaking. Sleep seemed to
have deserted me. I almost resolved to forsake forever fine
sheets, white walls, snug houses, comfortable feather beds
and once again take to the open air – but a wink of sleep
came upon me – just one little wink.

I was awakened suddenly.

I turned on my side and listened. It was evident something had struck the windows.

'Heavy rain,' I said to myself, 'but let the brown rain
pour down in torrents, for I'll not get out of bed today,' and I
pulled the bed-clothes more tightly about me.

I started to count lest sleeplessness should again assail
me. It did not, I fell asleep. Again the noise at the window!
What was it? I was too lazy to rise, almost too lazy to open
my eyes; but I could not help listening.

One cannot estimate time in one's sleep; I do not know
what time had elapsed when the noise came again. But it
came. I watched ...

Somebody was throwing sand at the window in order to
awaken me. I can assure you I did not give that person my
blessing.

I heard a woman's voice outside. I recognised the voice,
and as soon as I did I jumped out of bed; but I vow to you

45

that no other earthly sound could entice me from my fine bed at that early hour.

But that woman! Who would fail her?

# Daddo's Shilling

## Sigerson Clifford[*]

Daddo was my grandfather and Nan was my grandmother
and they lived in a small house wedged in the middle of the
forty other small houses of Turret Street. I lodged with them
because my parents also had a little house and ten children
to take the bare look off it. When my mother persuaded Nan
to take one of us to her house the old lady lined us all up on
the kitchen floor and scrutinised us as though we had
measles or small-pox or something.

'Wasn't God good and to send me only the one daughter,' she said turning us around to the light to see the colour
of our eyes.

Nan was a great believer in the virtues of a blue eye and
we must have been a sore disappointment to her, for the ten
of us had two brown eyes each and if we had a third eye that
would be brown too I suppose.

'I'll take Sonny,' she decided in the end. 'He has the look
of my own poor father about him.' I wasn't too pleased at the
compliment, for her own poor father had been no great
shakes. When he had a pint of poteen in him he always
marched off with a pike to attack the police-barracks, but he
always sobered up before he reached it. Indeed, the old
man's forays were a sore trial to me at school where the
fellows that didn't like me remembered the phrase, 'When
Tadg More captures the police-barracks,' which was another
way of saying never. If you weren't a warrior in our valley
there was scant respect for you and if you were the descendant of a half-warrior like Tadg More you were blamed often
enough for the foibles of your ancestors.

Daddo had so many ghost stories he must have been a ghost

[*] From *The Red-Haired Woman and other Irish Stories* by Sigerson
Clifford.

himself one time. I sat wide-eyed beside the fire listening to the exploits of the black dogs, headless men, women with two heads to make up for the men, death-coaches and banshees until in the end I was afraid to go to the well for water after dark.

'You'll frighten the foolish brown eyes out of the fledgling's head,' Nan warned him in Irish.

They always spoke Irish when they didn't want me to understand and that was the rock they perished on for the Master had walloped plenty of it into my skull from an early age. And, besides, the brand of English we favoured in the valley was half-Irish.

Every Friday night Daddo and Nan had a row over a shilling and that was the only kind of stinging-match that ever took place between them while I was living in the house.

On Fridays after dinner Daddo clapped the black wide-awake hat on his head, lit his pipe, grabbed his blackthorn stick and stumped off to the post office for his pension.

'Twould be facing bedtime before he used show up and a smell of porter from him that should kick down a goalpost. Nan would shoot out her hand before he had time to say, 'God bless all here'.

'I suppose the shilling is missing again this time, you little hedgehog,' she'd shrill.

'"Tisn't then, I hope,' by Daddo. 'I spent a white florin only on porter and I should have the other eight shillings safe in the cashbox for you, my bright love.'

But though he searched himself hard and Nan searched him harder still, no more than seven shillings was ever found.

He went up to bed then to snore like a sea-lion and Nan used turn to me.

'He's a bigger liar than Cromwell. Kneel down boyeen bawn, and we'll offer up the Rosary for him for he'll never get to Heaven on his own.'

And the following morning Daddo always went down to the pubs on the Main Street to squander the mysterious shilling on what he called his 'cure'.

In the end the missing shilling played so much on Nan's nerves that she could hardly sleep worrying over it. It was beginning to annoy me, too, for I prided myself on my cleverness as a searcher, but Daddo was too cute for the pair of us.

One fine Friday evening Nan sent me in search of Daddo with instructions to wheedle the hiding-place out of him and let her know. I found Daddo in Casey's Snug at bay before a pack of foaming pints of porter, and telling his stories to a laughing ring of admirers, who were decent enough not to expect entertainment for nothing. He came out of the snug when he saw me.

'What ails her now, garsoon?' he asked.

'She told me to find out where you hide the shilling, Daddo, and let her know,' I told him.

'Did she, faith?' said Daddo with a wink that nearly squeezed porter out of his eyelids.

'She did, Daddo,' I assured him. 'But even if you did tell me I wouldn't make her wise.'

'You're a good garsoon,' Daddo praised me: 'Here's a red penny for you now and run home and tell Nan I'll show her the hiding-place when Tadg More captures the police-barracks.'

Into the snug with him again as though he was being reared in it.

When he was in bed that night we searched his hat, clothes and boots but there was no trace of the shilling.

'I know him like the cat knows boiling milk,' said Nan, 'and he has that shilling on him somewhere.'

But in spite of her, Daddo was out of the house at ten o'clock the following morning and belting off for Main Street for a couple of hairs of the black dog.

Three years later Nan died. Daddo and myself were with her after the priest had gone when she whispered to him for the last time.

'Wisha, where used you hide the shilling on me, Daddo?' she asked.

Daddo pulled out his pipe and removed the cover from

it. He took her hand and a shilling fell from the bowl of the pipe into her palm. She closed her fingers over it and smiled up at him. Daddo wouldn't be too cute for her any more now.

# Death Be Not Proud

## John B. Keane*

The land meant everything to Mick Henderson. The cardinal rule of his long life was its preservation. Envious neighbours whose own land had become run down through neglect and laziness would have outsiders believe that he loved the land more than he loved his wife and certainly more than he loved his family. This was not so. He had been fond of his wife when he married. He had remained fond of her through storm and calm over the years and even now when the physical aspect of his marriage was becoming something of a memory he treasured her companionship in a way that only long attachment can foster.

He would have been hard put to explain his obsession with the land. His wife understood fully and there were others like himself in the valley who felt as he did. These would be silent, tight-lipped men, not without humour and not given to vindicating or modifying what would seem to be an extraordinary preoccupation with the soil.

At seventy Mick Henderson found himself in a quandary. Labour was becoming impossible to come by. Factories were shooting up like thistles in the nearby towns and cities. Whatever work-force was available in the area was almost completely absorbed. Even his regular workman had deserted him for lucrative shiftwork and a five-day week. The latter was something of a joke amongst the farming community. All the holdings supported herds of milch cows and during the heavy milking periods these needed constant attention.

Once when endeavouring to hire a workman Mick was asked if he would settle for a five-day week.

'You can have a one-day week in the winter,' Mick had

* From *Irish Short Stories* by John B. Keane.

told him, 'but until such time as we have a five-day cow there will be no five-day week.'

He had gone so far as to offer free Sundays during the peak periods and occasional days off for special events but there was no competing with the attractions of the factories. He cut down his herd to a manageable size although he was still heavily in debt from having put three sons and two daughters through boarding schools and colleges. There was another son, Mikey, named after himself, a black sheep of sorts, who disappeared one morning when he was barely sixteen after a vicious row regarding his attitude towards further schooling. That was nearly ten years before. Mick Henderson knew his son's address in England, knew he was doing well as a charge-hand in a Coventry factory, knew enough in fact to make Mikey feel downright uncomfortable if he ever suspected such paternal interest.

The others had no feeling for the land, no concern about it. On his seventieth birthday he had betaken himself to the city to consult with his eldest son, Maurice, who was a solicitor there. After listening carefully for over half an hour Maurice submitted his opinion.

'Your safest and your easiest course,' he said dispassionately, 'is to sell out and live here in Dublin or if city life has no appeal for you there is nothing to prevent you from buying a comfortable house in the country. The money you would make from the sale would clear your debts and leave you with more than sufficient to ensure a comfortable life for mother and yourself until the end of your days.'

His second son, Eddie, was a dentist. Married with two children, he operated from a small surgery attached to his home in the suburbs. Late as it was when Mick called he found Eddie up to his eyes in work. Very late that night they sat round the sitting room fire and talked about the land. It was impossible not to like Eddie and his wife but they had little to offer by way of a solution. They also felt that selling the land would be the best way out.

It was the third son, Martin, a civil servant, who supplied the obvious answer. Mick had a job finding his house in the sprawling, estate-cluttered northside of the metropolis. Snugly seated in the back seat of a taxi he passed row after row of newly-erected, two-storied houses. After numerous enquiries the eventually discovered the estate. Another search and they located the house. It stood amid hundreds of others which looked alike.

'How in the name of God does anyone live here?' he had asked undiplomatically when Martin and his wife met him at the door.

'You get used to it,' Martin said enjoying his father's innate rustic perplexity.

In spite of his first impression he was pleasantly surprised by the interior of the house. It had a heartening spaciousness in contrast to what he had expected.

'You have a fine home Martin,' he announced by way of conciliation.

'It's only a few hundred yards from the school,' Martin's wife said, 'and that's what really matters.'

After the usual preliminaries Mick settled down to the business of outlining his problems. Martin and his wife listened sympathetically while he explained about the new factories and the scarcity of labour.

'The last thing I want to do is sell it,' he finished.

'The logical thing as far as I can see is to bring Mikey back from Coventry,' Martin suggested.

'Will he want to come back?' Mick asked.

'I have no doubt that he will,' Martin assured him.

Mick Henderson considered this for some time. It was a thought that had always been at the back of his head. All he needed was someone, other than himself, to suggest it. He was aware that Martin and Mikey were as close as brothers could be despite the distance that separated them. In age there was hardly a year between them. It was to be expected, therefore, that Martin would put forward a strong case for the youngest brother. Mick Henderson decided that he would find out how forceful Martin's advocacy might be.

'That's all very fine,' he said disinterestedly, 'but has he the feel for the land?'

'Why wouldn't he?' Martin hastened to reply, 'he's your son isn't he?'

'You're my son and you have no feel for it. Neither have Maurice or Eddie.'

'Look,' Martin pleaded, 'Mikey is different. He's only good with his hands. He was a hopeless scholar. If you had kept him at home when he kicked off the traces that first time he'd know it all now and you wouldn't be worrying about labour.'

"'Tis easy be wise after the event,' Mick Henderson said. He suspected that Mikey might have the true feeling for the land but there was no way he could be certain. He resolved to probe further.

'What guarantee have I that he won't flog the farm as soon as I pass on?' he asked.

'That's a chance you'll have to take but let me tell you this. Mikey is hardly likely to flog it when it's going to be his livelihood. You know as well as I that he knew how to handle livestock. That time before he ran away he had no objection to working on the farm. What he objected to was school.'

'Agreed,' Mick Henderson returned, 'but there's many a young lad will volunteer for anything to escape school.'

'I happen to know,' Martin's tone was really serious now, 'that if he doesn't come home this year he won't come home at all.'

'Did he say this?'

'Yes.'

'Then I suppose I had better contact him. What if he says no?'

'That's one thing he won't say,' Martin assured him. After this conversation Mick Henderson had no doubt in his mind that Martin and Mikey had discussed the latter's position in depth. On his way home by train he had ample time to think. His one fear was that the land might be sold after his death but this would happen anyway if Mikey refused to come home. He remembered when the farm had been signed over to him by his own father. It has been a bright May morning close on forty years before. He had no idea what his father's business in the neighbouring town might be when he instructed him to tackle the black mare to

54

the family trap. By midday he was the legal owner of the land. He had in no way pressurised his father although he had dropped hints that he was thinking of getting married. It was somewhat different in his case. The true feeling for the land was there. His father knew this, knew that the green pastures to which he had devoted the best years of his life would be safe for another generation. It was so important that Mikey have this feeling for the acres which would shortly be under his care. Mick Henderson knew everything there was to be known about the land. Over the years he had discovered its idiosyncrasies and failings and learned painstakingly how to turn deficiencies into advantages. The land had its own unique characteristics, its own vague, imperceptible contours, its inexplicable portions of soft and hard, wet and dry, barren and lush.

On the surface the fields were like any other in the district but he knew better. His father had been a source of constant help as he endeavoured to discover the true lie of the land. Now that he knew all there was to be known it was high time the knowledge was passed on. He would announce his decision to his wife Julia as soon as he got home. She would be pleased. He was aware that she secretly pined after her youngest son although, like all mothers, she became somewhat resigned to his absence as time went by.

The proper thing for me to do, Mick thought, is to impress upon him without seeming to do so the value of well-treated land. I will show him that while human life is to be valued more than anything else, that which sustains it should be valued no less. I will pass over and my wife will pass over but the land will remain. We are only passing through, mere tenants at best. The land will be there forever to nurture my seed and the seed of my seed. Somehow he would try to get these feelings through to Mikey. If the genuine consciousness was there this would be no problem. If Mikey did not fully respond all would not be lost. At least he would not sell and the land would be saved. If one generation failed to throw up a man with love for the land the next generation was sure to compensate. Who could tell but he might live to see a grandson blessed with the appropriate and peculiar disposition so difficult to define.

Mikey Henderson arrived home during the second week of spring. The roadside hedgebanks were bright with clusters of early primroses and along the sides of the avenue leading to the old farmhouse were healthy clumps of daffodils and irises in various stages of flower. It was a good time to come home. During the first months he made many mistakes but Mick was not slow to notice that he never made the same mistake a second time. He was uncannily adept with all sorts of machinery. He understood cattle and most important of all he knew how to husband his strength. He fitted perfectly into the pattern of things.

Mick watched his progress with the keenest interest. Who knew but some evening he might see Mikey with his hands on his hips surveying the sheen of a freshly-ploughed tillage field or shading his eyes against a summer sun on the headland of a meadow ripe for cutting.

With the coming of summer the new green grass, luscious and fleecy, returned to the fields. The hedgerows no longer bare hosted a thousand songbirds and the first of the long herbage took the naked look from the broad meadows.

The meadows would prove to be the chief of Mikey's problems that first summer. It wasn't a particularly good year for growth. The new crops were light and late and to crown the general misfortune of the farming community there was no labour available when the outlook was favourable for harvesting. The weather too was unkind. To say the least it was inconsistent. Fine days were few and far between and rarely succeeded each other. During this time came the worst calamity that could possibly befall. Julia Henderson took ill and had to be removed to hospital. All thoughts of harvesting had to be abandoned until she recovered.

It was two weeks before she was released. She had undergone a mild coronary. Her doctor warned that unless she cut down considerably in her everyday work there would be a recurrence. After her short stay in the hospital she felt refreshed and the tiredness which had nagged her for so long seemed to have disappeared altogether. She herself declared that she felt twenty years younger and insisted in shouldering her full quota of chores. A young girl was found locally to help her. She agreed to stay until the schools reopened in September. Outwardly, at any rate, Julia Henderson seemed very much rejuvenated. She looked the picture of health and there was none of the breathlessness which she so often endured before her visit to hospital.

There was a general air of excitement all over the district when the weather changed for the better. Despite the fact that there was no immediate prospect of labour Mick and Mikey Henderson decided to make an all-out assault on the uncut meadows. All day they followed each other on two tractors. In their wake the tall grass fell in long parallel swathes. Julia and the girl brought their meals to the meadow. There was no tarrying for small-talk afterwards. As soon as they had eaten they mounted the cumbersome machines. The onslaught lasted until the first faint stars appeared in the late evening sky. The moment they finished they headed straight for the local pub. It wasn't that they especially needed a drink. It was the only place where they were likely to recruit labour. They were partly successful. It was first necessary to invest in several rounds of drink and to exhibit an interest in the welfare of likely prospects that was tantamount to fawning. This, with the offer of almost double the normal wage, was responsible for the extraction of three promises. Both Mick and Mikey were well aware that the trio in question were not exactly the cream of the crop. They would be late and they would put no great strain on themselves but they were labourers and if the weather held the produce of the combined meadows might be saved at the end of three days.

For most of the first day they turned and then tossed the freshly mown swathes. Late in the afternoon they made it up into wind-rows in preparation for the following day's cocking. This completed they broke off. That night the Hendersons listened avidly to the weather forecast. The prospects were still good. Mick and Mikey rose with the dawn. First the cows had to be milked. Then the milk had to be cooled and transported to the creamery. After that it was straight to the meadow. Everything else was secondary. The labourers arrived at ten o'clock and then the business of cocking commenced. First the crisp hay had to be gathered by the tractor-drawn, iron-toothed rake. Mikey attended to this particular function. He worked furiously supplying the needs of the cock-makers who worked in pairs. When the supply exceeded the demand he would jump from the tractor and shoulder huge pikefuls of hay to the base of the developing cock. This was the hardest part of haymaking. One by one, slowly and painfully, the cocks went up until by the end of the second day half the entire crop was safe. The third day followed the same pattern as the second. The mid-day meal was brought to the meadow by Julia Henderson and the girl. On the third day Julia came alone. The girl had not showed up. Enquiry revealed that she had been at a dance the night before and was unable to get out of bed. Julia was not unprepared. She arrived at the meadow shortly after noon, just as the sky was undergoing a murky suffusion in the southwest. If rain was to come this would be the direction from which it would threaten. After the meal one of the labourers announced that he was unable to continue because of a stomach ailment. Mick guessed that the pace was not to his liking. The same man had shown himself to be somewhat of a shirker from the beginning. Mikey had heard him derogatorily remarking to one of his colleagues that if he was to die he wouldn't like it to be for a farmer.

Despite her husband's protestations Julia insisted in falling in by his side. They worked together, silently, at a corner of the meadow far removed from the other pair. Julia Henderson was the ideal farmer's wife. Always she had been by her husband's side when the need was there. Of solid farming stock herself. She was aware of her obligations al-though these had often ranged from milking the entire herd to deputising at weddings and funerals. This was the un-written law when labour was not to be had.

Now and then Mick would glance anxiously to the west and south where the ominous turgescence of massing clouds was slowly enveloping the otherwise clear sky. By his own reckoning he estimated that there were three, maybe four good hours left. Given that much time all the hay would undoubtedly be saved. He redoubled his own efforts and then without warning of any kind Julia Henderson heaved a massive, choking sigh. Mick stood helpless and appalled while she attempted to restrain with clutching fingers the terrible upheaval in her chest. Then just as suddenly her hands fell listlessly to her sides and she fell backwards noiselessly in a crumpled heap. Urgently Mick Henderson bent and whispered an act of contrition into her ear. There was no disputing the fact that she was dead. He stretched her legs gently and folded her hands across her bosom.

Then he sat by her side awaiting the arrival of Mikey with the next rake of hay. The young man sensed that something was wrong. He dismounted slowly from the tractor and read the news in his father's face. He knelt by his mother's side and kissed her on the lips and forehead. He smoothed back the hair from her face and lifted her head so that he could rest it on the pillow of hay. Then he rose and looked at the sky.

'Let's get on with it,' he said. At first Mick Henderson looked at him uncomprehendingly. Then the logic of it dawned on him.

'What about the two?' he asked, pointing to where the labourers were building a cock at the other end of the meadow.

'What they don't know won't trouble them,' said Mikey dismissing the question. Slowly his father rose. Already Mikey was adding to the half-made cock. Instinctively his father followed his example.

Before departing for another rake-up Mikey laid a hand on his father's shoulder.

'She would understand,' he said. 'I don't have to tell you that. When the job is done we'll take her indoors. Then I'll go for a priest.'

So saying he mounted the machine and in a matter of seconds was again raking the ever-decreasing wind-rows. Mick Henderson cast a glance at his dead wife and then his eyes followed his youngest son. Beyond doubt here was a man with a sound sense of values, a man with a true feel for the land.

# The Horse Thieves of Ballysaggert

## Brian Cleeve[*]

Sorrow, is it? I tell you, if a man were wanting to make a list of the Chief Sorrows of Erin, I'd advise him to give great consideration to the Sorrow of Ballysaggert, ever since the day Sergeant Raftery found Uncle Jamesy's still up in the Fairy Fort. The best poteen that ever a man could wish to drink this side of heaven was distilled up there by Uncle Jamesy and my father, while now – now you wouldn't wet your whistle with a drop that hadn't paid excise duty in the four corners of Ballysaggert parish. And all over a horse. A sway-backed vagrant of a four-legged monstrosity that ought to have been sent to a glue factory when it was born. But let me tell you in proper order.

The real beginning of the whole miserable business was the coming of Sergeant Raftery to replace old Sergeant Kieron that retired. A new police sergeant is always a hard business for a parish, the way he'll be bursting out all over with enthusiasm and ambition. But this feller. Like a maniac. A huge, ugly man with red hair growing out of his ears, and hands like bats of lumpy wood, and a savagery for work that would have killed an Eskimo. There was hardly an hour of the day or night you wouldn't find him ravaging and stravaging the roads looking for mischief to make. Impounding donkeys that knew their way home better than he did, or looking for dog licenses, or rounding up truants until the schoolhouse was a bedlam with imprisoned children that the teacher hardly knew by sight and didn't want to.

Stars in heaven, there wasn't any ruffianism that ser-

---

From *The Horse Thieves of Ballysaggert and Other Stories* by Brian Cleeve.

geant wasn't up to. And, of course, he wasn't ten days in the place before he heard about the still. Not where it was, of course, or who owned it. Just that it existed. But that was enough. From that out, high days and holidays, he'd be quartering the mountains like a sixteen-stone greyhound, looking for a wisp of smoke to tell him where the still was.

And then, after about a month of all this torment and turmoil, when half the lads in the parish, including myself, were thinking of emigrating, didn't I see a girl I'd never seen before in all my life? A girl? A living vision. My heart turned over and my mouth fell open with the beauty of her and I had to lean against the nearest house wall to stop myself from falling down flat while she walked toward me, with the sunlight sprinkling gold dust on her curling black hair and her little red hat. Walked, did I say? Danced. Floated. Her foot no more than kissed the ground as she went by me, and I fetched a sigh out of me that nearly brought my heart along with it.

She just nodded to me and smiled, and said, 'Good morning,' and was gone down the street, like a feather dancing on a puff of breeze, while I lay against the whitewashed wall of Matt Fogarty's cottage and wondered if I was alive or dead.

I just wandered up to the still as lost and dazzled in my mind as if I was coming away from it instead of going toward it. Indeed, I was hit so bad that I spent five minutes trying to get into the wrong Fairy Fort.

Maybe I should explain that up beyond the head of the valley, where the mountain top flattens out, there's half a dozen biggish green mounds built by the good people in the old times. You'll hear all kinds of stories about them being graves of Kings and such, but that's all just foolish talk. They're Fairy Forts, and the only human thing ever buried in any of them was our still. A long while ago, when Uncle Jamesy and father were about my age, some professors came down from Dublin and started digging the forts to pieces. Looking for old pots and bones.

They left behind them a powerful big hole in the side of one of the forts, and down under it weren't there two great rooms all lined with stone, like a pair of cellars, hidden there under the green roof of the mound?

Uncle Jamesy and father said it was plain to see that whoever had built the rooms had been making no use of them for a power of years, and it'd be a sin to waste them. You wouldn't find as good a place as that to hide a poteen still if you searched all the provinces of Ireland.

And so they brought in their gear and set it up, and what with old Sergeant Kieron and Father Sweeney liking a drop of the poteen themselves an odd time, the still never had to be moved in thirty years. All the customers needed to do to come in was to grasp a particular dead furze stump sticking out of the side of the mound and lift it. Up it would come with a trap door covered in green turf attached to it, and down he'd step into what you might call the Saloon Bar of the Fairy Fort; a big, shadowy cave of a place with benches along three sides of it, and a barrel and a row of mugs on a shelf at the far end. Behind the barrel was a small, narrow passage leading to the second stone room, the stillroom itself.

Above both rooms, of course, was a stone roof, made of big overlapping slabs of rock. And over that again was the green turf of the mound, half covered in furze and bracken, with the smoke of the still curling out of a small chimney hidden in a gorse bush and losing itself in the gray, watery sky. I can tell you the heart nearly breaks in me for thinking of the homeliness of it all. Not having a mother since before I can remember, I more or less grew up in the still instead of down in father's cottage.

As I say, after seeing the girl below in Ballysaggert village, I was so bad I near dislocated my shoulder trying to pull up a furze stump on the wrong mound. And when I got into the still at last, it didn't take Uncle Jamesy long to see that something was up with me. He's a little, sharp-eyed man, the twin of my father, with tufts of white hair sprouting out over his ears and not another screed of it on his brown, shiny skull. And what with the way he and father sit cross-legged, from the long years of squatting under the copper condensing tube of the still filling jugs, and with near living in the Fairy Fort, it's not much wonder that everyone calls the pair of them the leprechauns. Indeed, they're known as the leprechauns far and wide beyond Ballysaggert.

'Michael boy,' my uncle said, before I could so much as settle myself on the bench. 'What have you been doing?'

'Nothing,' I said dreamily.

'You've been after girls,' said my uncle, the end of his nose twitching. He's always been powerfully against women, saying they were the ruin of a man's drinking habits. 'I know it. I know it. I can see it in your eye. Oh, Michael child, if you only knew the depths of the pit that's opening at your innocent feet. Girls is the calamity of mankind.'

He filled himself a mug and took a sup of it as if he needed strengthening. Meanwhile, I must confess, I didn't pay much heed to him beyond blushing a bit. I could still see her in my mind's eye. The little dancing foot of her, as neat as a new leaf fluttering on a tree. The print of it was on my heart.

'It's your father's fault,' Uncle Jamesy said. 'He's never taught you the facts of life. Girls is innocent enough, I'll grant you that, for dallying and dandling. Like kittens. But girls become women the way kittens become cats, and then where are you? There isn't the like of a woman for devilment in the world wide.' He drained the mug and gave his hands a little wring together. 'I was telling your father only the other day that it was time one of us did be warning you ...'

A shaft of sunlight fell between us then, and it was my father himself coming in with a sack of potatoes for the still.

'By the Lord,' he said, 'I've just heard the worst news I ever heard.'

'Then you've heard the same thing that I have,' said Uncle Jamesy. 'The boy there has started tricksying after girls –'

'Arrah go on with you and your girls,' said my father. 'This is serious. The sergeant has got himself a horse.'

'What of it?' said Uncle Jamesy. 'If he took to fox hunting now, wouldn't it be the good thing for us, although heaven have mercy on the poor horse that man puts his leg across.'

'You don't understand,' said father. 'It isn't foxes he's going to be hunting. It's us. And whereas he wouldn't catch so much as old Mary O'Mahony on his two great feet, with them sinking into the bog twelve inches deep at every step, on horseback he'll have the legs of every man of us.'

'You have something there,' said my uncle, beginning to look very grave.

'I wish I hadn't,' said my father. 'But how many times has he nearly caught one or other of the lads as it is, and him with maybe a bottle of poteen in his coat pocket and a breath on him strong enough to light your pipe at? And once he has one of them caught and murdered with questions it won't be long before we have to give this place back to them we borrowed it from.' And he jerked his thumb at the saucer in the corner, where there was always a sup of poteen laid out for the landlords. I never actually saw one of them drinking it, of course, and I don't believe in that kind of thing any more than you do, but it's certainly astonishing how every morning that saucer used to be dry. Dry as a cat would lick it, although we had no cat.

'Ruin,' said my father, 'that's what this means. It'll be like the Tans again.'

'The Tans?' said my uncle. 'I doubt even the Tans wouldn't have thought of a thing like this.'

Just on that, two of the lads came in for a drop of support after the day's work, and it was one of them, Peter Lowry, that brought the whole ruin down on us with his cleverality, once he heard what was up.

'Gob,' says he. 'Is that all that's troubling you? A horse?'

'Aye,' says my father. 'Isn't it enough? The talk is he's gone and bought it out of his own money, the policemen up in Dublin not thinking it necessary to put a horse on the establishment. But he reckons that once he has the still found and a dozen or so arrests made they'll buy him a motorcar, let alone a horse.'

'Better'n betterer,' said Peter Lowry, twisting his long red nose in his fingers and squinting very cunning at us under the peak of his cap. 'He won't be in the mood to buy a second horse out of his money, hardly.'

'What are you getting at?' said my uncle.

'Stealing the horse, of course,' shouted Peter. 'Down to his house one dark night, pocket full of sugar. Tsk, tsk and out comes the horse, ready to follow you to Kingdom Come for the sugar lumps. And I know a lad over Killnoggin way would buy anything on four legs and no questions asked.' He laid his finger alongside of his nose and winked the way you'd think he had something in his eye.

As maybe you can tell, I've never forgiven Peter Lowry for any of this, and neither has anyone else in the parish. But, of course, we hadn't the means of telling future woe from present stupidity, and the plan certainly sounded reasonable enough. Except that it turned out that what with being a mountainy man and not used to horses, Peter Lowry wouldn't be able for stealing the horse himself. For a moment or two it looked like the plan being dropped, when didn't it come into my uncle's head to mention about me looking moony over a girl?

'A girl, is it?' said Peter. 'It wouldn't be a girl you saw today for the first time? A little dark-haired bit of a thing tittuping along the street just now?'

I gaped at him with my mouth open, and a blush coming up from my shirt collar to my cap, wondering how he knew. Although for the matter of that, I shouldn't have been surprised. There was never anything concerning other people in Ballysaggert that Peter Lowry didn't have his nose stuck into sooner or later, and usually sooner.

'The sergeant's daughter,' he said, slapping his knee again. 'No other in the world wide. Philomena, her name is. Working over in Killnoggin in a grand draper's shop till me bold sergeant sent for her to mind house for him. Did you speak to her, Michael?'

I shook my head. The sergeant's daughter! If he'd said the devil's daughter I couldn't have been more amazed. But 'Philomena'. Did you ever hear a more beautiful name than that?

'You didn't speak to her yet?' Peter was saying. 'Then don't be wasting any more time, boy. Court her, and flatter her. Whisper to her in the moonlight. And if you don't have the key of the sergeant's stable door out of her inside a week you're not the lad I take you for.' He turned to my uncle and my father. 'There's your man for you. There's the lad will steal the horse.'

'But I don't know anything about horses either,' I said.

'Ah,' said Peter. 'But a lad like you will know about girls, and that's what's important here.'

'Don't be listening to him, Michael,' said my uncle. 'Don't be tempting the child, Peter Lowry. Nothing but ill and harm could come of it.'

'Wait now,' said my father, beginning to look thoughtful. 'Maybe something might come of it, at that. Don't be so hasty, James, telling the lad what he'll do and not do. It might be no harm if the lad sounded out the grounds, so to speak.'

'Ruin,' said Uncle Jamesy, wringing his hands. 'There was never a plan yet with a woman in it that didn't end in ruin. I'm warning you, Paudeen O'Shaughnessy,' Paudeen being my father's name.

'You and your warnings,' said Peter. 'Sure, aren't we facing ruin as it is?'

'Peter's right,' said my father. 'Let you see what you can do, Michael child. Although, anything you do, keep your mind on the horse. Remember, the girl is only ways and means.'

'There's the man,' said Peter, refilling his mug without so much as a by-your-leave. 'The thing is as good as done.'

Even so, there was none of us except Peter Lowry that wasn't more than doubtful about the whole plan. And if I entered into it at all it wasn't for the sake of the horse, I can tell you that. But before a week had passed we had the doubts driven out of us. The Tans? Mounted on his brute of a horse, the sergeant was more like Cromwell and his cavalry destroying the countryside. You could hardly move on the mountain without the terror of the hoofs thundering behind you.

The one salvation of us in that week was that the sergeant wasn't much of a fist at riding. And time and again

66

when he near had one of us ridden down with the poteen turning our legs to water and a bottle of the darling stuff maybe clutched to our chests to keep out the night chill, wouldn't he fall off with a tremendous splash into a bog hole? But as the days passed, either he got better at riding, or the horse at being ridden, and on Saturday night didn't my father himself have the nearest squeak of his life, trotting over to Father Sweeny's presbytery with a half-gallon jar.

'Things can't go on like this much longer,' he said to me in a voice that was still trembling the next morning. 'You're the one hope we have left, Michael child. How is the plan progressing?'

To tell you the truth the horse side of it hadn't progressed very far. But the other side of it was fair rampaging along. We'd got to the stage where we met every night under the big oak tree beyond the crossroads, and I was repairing the gaps in my education left by my being brought up by my uncle and my father, with no female influence about the place. I was staggered at how much there was to learn. And of course, in the midst of it all I couldn't help learning a little bit about the horse. The sergeant kept it locked in a shed at the bottom of the garden when he wasn't scouring the countryside on its back, and he kept the key hanging in his kitchen. Moreover, after dark, either he or his daughter was always in the house. She could only meet me when he was taking a nap after his supper, with the key hanging a bare two feet from his big, ugly ear. It didn't seem possible to get near it.

And then, that very morning, didn't the whole thing fall into my lap?

'Michael,' whispered Philomena as I was passing her at the corner of the chapel wall. 'I can't be meeting you tonight, after all. Father'll be over in Killnoggin till late this evening, and I have to mind the house. I wouldn't dare leave it empty in case he found out.' And as she spoke I saw like a flash of lightning what I had to do. I took her little white hand and squeezed it.

'I'd die, passing a whole night without seeing you,' I said, and true enough for me I would have too. 'Why shouldn't I come and see you in the house itself?'

'Oh, you'd never,' she gasped, blushing like a rose in the snow. But something in her eyes didn't look as shocked as her voice sounded, and I just gave her a wink and her little warm hand another squeeze, and went off up the road, whistling. And not all because of the horse either.

I think that Sunday was the longest day of my life. But it ended at last, and the shadows were hardly falling before I was down to the sergeant's back door. At the end of the garden I could hear the horse shuffling and scuffling in its shed, and inside the house Philomena singing like a black-bird about the kitchen.

'Ah,' says I, 'I'll have you both where I want you before the evening's out.' And I tilted my cap and tapped on the door. 'It's me, Michael,' I whispered. 'Open up to me, my darling.'

And there was her little rosy lips at the crack of the door, begging to be kissed by a lad sensible enough not to listen to her saying 'no'. In I squeezed, and if you want to know about the next half hour it isn't me that'll be telling you. But everything good has an end, as they say, and after one last little kiss I made pretend I heard her father coming. By this time, of course, the key of the shed was well in my own pocket, unbeknownst to Philomena.

'I'll just slip out and look,' I said. So out with me long enough to unlock the shed, then back into the kitchen again. 'All clear as yet,' I said, clasping her in my arms and hanging the key on its hook again behind her back, while her mind was otherwise occupied. 'But I'd better be going, even so.'

It was as easy as that, misfortune to me. Half an hour and a pound of lump sugar later I was leading the horse up to the trap door of the fort.

'Psst,' I said. 'I have him.' Father and Uncle Jamesy came out to look.

'Why in the name of heaven didn't you tell us you were going to do it tonight, you stupid gawn?' said my father.

'What are we going to do with it till Peter Lowry comes? And even then he has to fetch his friend. Where are we going to hide a thing that size and the sergeant tearing down the mountains to look for it?'

I hadn't thought of any of that, but I was inspired that night. There was the horse blowing down my neck, looking for more sugar. And there was the black mouth of the open trap door into the side of the Fairy Fort.

'In there,' I said. 'Five minutes' work with a spade round the sides of the trap door will make a hole big enough for him, and when we've eased him inside the fort and put the sods of turf back again, the head of all the police in Ireland wouldn't guess there was a horse hidden in there.'

And after a bit of argument with Uncle Jamesy, that's what we did. Inside of an hour we had the horse as snug inside the still as if it was in its own stable. Snugger indeed, for I'll guarantee the sergeant never gave it mashed potatoes to eat, nor a bucket of second-run poteen to drink, to keep it quiet and happy while it was waiting for Peter Lowry's friend.

But there was no rest for me. I had to be down to the village again to look for Peter Lowry, who was courting a girl there on his own account. And that was how I ran into trouble. I hadn't set foot in the village street before I saw the sergeant rampaging along, practically carrying poor Philomena by the scruff of her neck.

'Where is it then?' he was roaring. 'Where is the blasted horse if you never left eyes off of it? Out, you've been, that's what. Skylarking and gallivanting and courting in the lanes like a strumpet.' And he lifted her till her feet swung off the ground, and shook her like a dog shaking a little, warm, wee rabbit. My blood near boiled in my heart and if I'd been a foot taller and fifty pounds heavier I'd have up and struck him, Philomena's father or no. But that moment, just as I was melting back into the darkness, didn't Philomena see me?

'Michael,' she wailed. 'There's Michael O'Shaughnessy, father. He'll tell you. Did I ever leave the house this whole night, Michael?'

And before I knew where I was, *my* feet were off the ground and *I* was being shaken like a rabbit. One of us in either hand. He's a terribly big man is the sergeant. 'What do

69

you know about my horse, Michael O'Shaughnessy?' he said in a police-court voice.

'Nothing,' I said. 'I never laid eyes on it. Did you lose it?'

'I did,' he said, sounding very grim. 'But I won't be long in finding it nor the blackguards that did it. Get home with you, girl,' he said, putting Philomena down on one side of him and me on the other, and producing a bull's-eye lantern. I made to follow Philomena, but he grabbed me again.

'You come with me,' he said. 'I've an idea you know something more of this business than appears.'

So I went with him, while he shone the torch on the road and along the verge till he saw a place where the horse had left fresh hoofprints in the mud and wet grass, just where I'd led the horse off the road an hour or so before. Which was another thing I hadn't thought of. From then on, it was like following a path.

Straight to the trap door like a line of broad arrows went the horse's hoofprints, and the sergeant after them with me trailing along side him.

'I think they go up that-a-way,' I suggested, pointing away from the fort.

'Do you?' said the sergeant. 'Well, I don't then. I think they go this-a-way.' And he came to the green, sloping side of the fort itself, and lifted his foot to climb up and over it, thinking of course, that the trail he was following must go over it too.

And that very second, hearing my voice, and thinking the second voice must be Peter Lowry's didn't father open the trap door? Heavens above, it was like a thing you'd see in the films. The black hole appearing suddenly in the side of the Fairy Fort, father's head popping up out of it like a bald rabbit, and the sergeant bringing his size-fourteen boot down on top of it as if he was using it for a stepping-stone. I never saw two men look more startled in my mortal life. Down went father as if he'd been shot in the skull. Down went the sergeant plunging on top of him through the open trap door. And up from the still came the most catastrophic crashing and whinnying you'd hear outside of a collapsing stable. Because, of course, the horse was underneath.

Holding my breath, I went to the edge of the trap to look. And there, looking like the devils roasting in hell in the bit of lamplight, was father lying in one corner of the still, Uncle Jamesy in another, and right in the middle the sergeant draped over the horse's rump, and the horse staggering to and fro and shaking its ugly head as if it couldn't believe what was going on, which I suppose it couldn't. One more sway and the sergeant slid to the ground, and just in the same second the horse let a lash out of his back foot that would have broken another man's skull. Even with the sergeant it laid him as cold as a daisy under the poteen barrel. Finally, the horse itself buckled at the knees, gave a kind of small groan of bewilderment and despair, laid its head on the sergeant's stomach, and went to sleep.

'Gob,' said father, sitting up and feeling himself. 'Are we dead?' Then he felt Uncle Jamesy and sat him up. 'Are you all right there, Jamesy?'

'It's the girl,' said Uncle Jamesy, feeling round for the mug he'd been drinking out of when he got knocked into the corner. 'I said no good would come of anything with a girl involved in it. Didn't I say that, Paudeen? But none of you would listen to me. And now the still is ruined on us.'

'Oh, come up out of that,' I whispered. 'It won't be only the still that'll be ruined if you stay there arguing the toss. The sergeant'll have the life out of all of us. Put your hand on his heart and see is he breathing.'

'Breathing?' said Uncle Jamesy. 'He's snoring like a traction engine. Come down here out of that and give us a hand shifting the still.'

Because, of course, with the sergeant lying there in the middle of the Fairy Fort there wasn't much point in leaving things for him when he came to himself again. And so for the next hour and a half we hefted and humped and shifted every blessed bit of the still up out of the fort and away down to Peter Lowry's shed. Finally we took away the trap door and dug the hole bigger and ragged all round to make it look as if the horse had fallen into the fort of his own accord. By the time we'd finished, you could have gone over the place with a currycomb and not found so much as the peeling of a potato to hint that there's ever been a spoonful of poteen concocted inside it. And still the sergeant and the horse lay draped across each other in the middle of the floor, like two big, ugly logs. Only the horse had the most queer expression on its face, sort of smiling dreamily in its sleep. And it suddenly struck me to wonder why the horse was asleep at all.

'Because it's drunk, of course,' said Uncle Jamesy bitterly, when I asked him. 'Blind drunk. And why wouldn't it be after two buckets of poteen, and near kicking in the barrel to get the second one? It was the only thing would keep the brute quiet. Oh, this is a sad, bad day for Ballysaggert.'

It must have been a pretty sad day for the sergeant, too, when he woke up and found his evidence gone from around him. And sadder still for him when he got the three of us into court over in Killnoggin a week later. He wouldn't have brought us within ten miles of the law, of course, on the sort of story he had to tell, only for the kick he'd had, and the blind rage he was in because of the way things had gone. I think it must have left him kind of muzzy-minded for a while. Indeed, it was only in the courtroom itself, and him on the witness stand giving his evidence, with a big square of plaster stuck on his head, that you could see him coming to his senses. He'd hardly begun about his horse when things started to look bad for him.

'You went to look for your horse in a Fairy Fort,' said the justice, beginning to sound rather grim.

'No, justice,' the sergeant said, 'it was only when the fort opened under my foot and I fell in on top of one of the leprechauns that I found the horse was there –'

'One of the lep – one of the leprechauns?' said the justice very slowly. There was a big yell of laughter from some of the lads at the back of the courtroom, and I saw the sweat starting on the sergeant's forehead like marbles.

'I mean one of the defendants, your honour,' he said miserably, as if he knew that he was a lost man from then on. 'The people about call them the leprechauns because of the way they look.'

The justice peered at us over his spectacles, where we lined up, and we all tried to look as unleprechaunlike as three innocent men could.

'Go on,' said the justice, but you could tell that he wasn't feeling very well disposed to the sergeant.

'Then the horse kicked me in the head, your honour, and when I woke up wasn't the whole place dismantled and gone, and me lying there in the middle of the floor of the fort with the roof of it gaping to the sky above my head –'

'And you suggest that the leprechauns had taken everything away during the night?' asked the justice in a very silky kind of voice.

'Yes, justice,' roared the sergeant like a bull with dogs round him; and at that the yell of laughter from the lads near lifted the roof.

'Case dismissed,' said the justice, pounding on the desk in front of him with his little wooden hammer.

For father and Uncle Jamesy it was as total a victory as a pair of honest men could wish. They even had a new place for the still; a little, disused quarry far back in the mountains where the sergeant could be looking a year without finding it. But for myself, I was more concerned about how I could face Philomena after what we'd just done to her father. And there she was, right in the middle of the path outside the courthouse, wringing her darling hands.

'Oh, Michael,' she said, before I could sneak off, and then she was in my arms, sobbing her heart out on my shoulder. 'Did you hear what they're saying about him?' she wailed. 'That he was drunk. Father! That never touched a drop in his life except at Christmas.'

'There, there,' I said, patting her head, and steering her out of the High Street into the peace and quiet of a little lane that led down beside the river. 'There, there.' And somehow we got off the subject of her father altogether, which was just as well. Because the things we got to talking about needed a lot less explaining on my part.

But up at the quarry, father and Uncle Jamesy couldn't have enough of it, laughing their heads off over the way the sergeant had looked in court, and how he was wasting his time traipsing and traipsing over the countryside again on his sway-backed monstrosity of a horse.

But the evening of the third day they stopped laughing pretty abruptly when the horse came stepping down into the quarry and pushed his big ugly head right inside the shaft where they had the still, snuffling with delight at the smell of the poteen. He'd got a taste for the stuff up in the Fairy Fort, and the second he'd got within half a mile of the quarry, down had gone his head and snuff, snuff, snuff, like a blessed dog rather than a horse, hadn't he smelled them out? They only got out of jail barely in time for the wedding, between me and Philomena.

And I can tell you, there wasn't much poteen drunk to celebrate that event, nor hasn't been since. Because once the sergeant realised that horse of his could smell out a still, what did he do but turn the creature into a kind of flying column, laying waste the countryside on all sides. There isn't a still left hardly, between Killnoggin and the sea. There's even talk now of him being promoted to inspector, on the Poteen Squad. My own father-in-law, and me the descendant of untold generations of poteen-makers! I don't know how I'll ever live down the shame.

# Part Two:

# The Story Tellers

# *from* The Tailor and Ansty

## Eric Cross

'In the townland of Garrynapeaka, in the district of Inchi-
geela, in the parish of Iveleary, in the barony of West Muskerry, in the county of Cork, in the province of Munster' –
as he magniloquently styles his address, lives the Tailor.

His small whitewashed cottage, with its acre of ground,
stands at the brow of a hill, at the side of a road which winds
and climbs into a deep glen of the mountains bordering
Cork and Kerry.

In the summer you will usually find the Tailor himself
leaning up against the bank of the road, minding his one
black cow. As you pass up the hill he will have watched you
come and sized you up in his shrewd and kindly way. As he
stands talking to you, helping you, pointing out this and that
to you, you will scarcely believe that he has seventy-seven
years put over him. The vigour of his body, in spite of the
handicap of his crutch, the firm tones of his voice, the smile
of his lively eyes, the thick head of silver hair, all belie the
fact of the years.

He will most likely invite you inside for a glass of
buttermilk or a heat of the tea. Go with him. Let the beauties
of Ireland wait. They will still be there when he has gone. Be,
as he is, prodigal of time, and sit and listen to him. Forget
the rest of your journey as the Tailor forgets the cow.
Humanity matters more than either cattle or scenery. You
have met a man – finished.

Sit by his turf fire at night and learn how to practise his
favourite precept – 'Glac bog an saoghal agus glachgig an
saoghal bog tu: Take the world fine and aisy and the world
will take you fine and aisy.' And that other one of his: 'The
world is only a blue bag. Knock a squeeze out of it when you
can.'

You have met a man who has lived to the utmost within
his limits. A man who has grown and learned and become

wise and splendidly tolerant and full of a sense of fun. Someone whom St Francis, Montaigne, Rabelais, Shakespeare and his Falstaff would have loved – richly human. First of all human, and the rest – Irish, Catholic, tailor – afterwards.

Always he has suffered the handicap of a withered leg and has hobbled through life with a crutch and a stick. He has treated that as a mere bagatelle and brushed it aside with an air of contemptuous indifference as he has treated so many of the details of life. Actually, indeed, it has proved little handicap to his activity. He has managed to find his way all over the mountains of West Cork and Kerry. He has travelled distances by road which would tire a strong man with two sound legs. He has managed to travel beyond his own country, and still at seventy-seven clambers up the rocks of his little acre for a vantage-point for the herding of his cow.

Now he does little travelling. 'The heart is playing at him.' His journeyings are limited to Garrynapeaka apart from an occasional excursion by car. He does not worry. Garrynapeaka is a mirror of the rest of the world. The road runs through it, and those who travel the road – neighbours on their way to a fair, the local guards, visitors in the summer – all drop into him. On winter nights his kitchen is always full. He learns all the news, all the gossip, all the scandal, and what happens in Iveleary is, after all, of deeper concern to him than the doubtful headline reports from Outer Mongolia which we call news. He is content now to be a great traveller in Garrynapeaka, as another wise man was 'content to have travelled much in Concord'.

He has received an old age pension of ten shillings a week since he was seventy. He takes great glee in the fact that, to date, he has managed to get £150 from the Government 'free, gratis and for nothing'. He remarks on the fact that his mother lived to be ninety-eight, and if she had been drawing 'the pension' she would have drawn over seven hundred pounds! He chuckles at the possibility of his own achievement of that age. It is not the greed for money. He is contemptuous of money. It is the sense of fun of the thing.

Though he is tailor by trade as well as by name to all who know him, he has not practised the craft seriously for many years. But his interest in the trade remains. He will offer 'to build a suit' for you, but you would need the patience of Job to see the end of the job. He will study the cut of your clothes. He will finger the stuff of which they are made, and his tradesman's pride is roused at the sight of a missing button.

He will readily offer to put a stitch in something for you, or to sew on a button or to patch a wearing garment. The job, however, will be incidental to the talk. He will hold you a prisoner by a needle and thread or to ransom in your shirt sleeves. The button sewing may take an hour's combined labour and talk. A puckish sense of fun runs through it all. If it should be an alpaca jacket which is at fault the Tailor will invariably patch it with a piece of broadcloth. If the missing button is black you may be certain that the one he sews on will be white. In his own phrase – 'They serve the purpose. What harm?'

He can be serious withal, and give a considered opinion or discuss any topic you may care to introduce. But life is too short for a long face. Soon his eyes will twinkle, the corners of them will wrinkle, his lips will tremble and he will burst into a chuckle which grows to a rollicking, room-filling laugh at the thought of some incident which has invaded and tickled his mind.

'Keep all the fun to yourself, of course!' breaks in the scornful voice of Ansty.

Ansty is the obverse of the medal – The Tailor and Ansty. She is his wife or, as he refers to her, 'his bitter half, his misfortune'. In almost all aspects they differ, yet each is incomplete without the other. They are Jack Spratt and his wife. Between them they lick the platter of life clean.

The Tailor finds some good content in the worst day of the winter. Ansty finds some fault in the best day that the summer ever brings. The Tailor sits, Silenus-like, upon his butter-box by the side of the fire, with fun and interest dancing in his eyes. Ansty wanders in and out of the house, broom in hand, hair awry, looking like one of the Furies and acting as an antithetical chorus to the Tailor's view of life.

The Tailor greets you at first sight with warmth. Not so Ansty. For a long time she will view you with a searching and sceptical eye. The Tailor treats the dog and cat as friends and talks to them. Ansty spends half her day hunting them with her broom, and cursing them with her tongue. If they are in they ought to be out. If they are out they ought to be in.

'Pigs where hens ought to be. Hens where pigs ought to be. Ten o'clock in the morning, and not a child washed yet in the house. The whole world is upside down!' comments the Tailor with mock wonder from his corner.

Again, the fire is always too big and wasteful for Ansty, or else too small and miserable. For the Tailor – there's a fire on the hearth. 'God's in His heaven. All's right with the world.'

The Tailor is interested in everything under the sun, and his mind, like a bee, sucks the nectar of every notion, whereas Ansty is interested in nothing but her immediate surroundings and the echoes which linger in her mind without interest. The Tailor will return tomorrow to a point discussed today with a freshly remembered instance or a pertinent story. He has a sense of continuity and flow. Ansty's thought and interest are a series of full stops and exclamations. An hour after a subject has been mentioned, she echoes a phrase of it, inconsequentially as she wanders in and out of the cottage:

'Domson wine! ... The Lord save us! ... Domson wine! ... Glory be! ... Domson wine! ... Ring a dora! Domson wine! ... Iosa Christe!'

The Tailor pauses in his discourse and cocks his ear for a moment, and then turns to Ansty with a serious inquiry.

'Tell me – is that a new saint that you and the Pope made this morning, that you are so busy saying your prayers to?'

Ansty, by the way, is an abbreviation of Anastasia, and the Tailor's official name is 'Mr Buckley', but they are known always as 'The Tailor and Ansty'.

Ansty has a hard life, made even harder by her own

nature. Most of the work of the place falls upon her, and her overture to most of the day's reminiscences begins with, 'Wisha! when I got up this morning, very early entirely, to let out the cow, and himself still shno–o–o–ring away in the bed like an ould pig, or a gintleman –'

Her life is a round of worries. She is at the mercy of every most trivial circumstance. She is full of fears for her ducks and hens from the passing motors and the fox and the rats. The rabbits will destroy the cabbage in the garden. The rain will destroy the turf. Then when all these everyday worries are banished there still remain the thunders and the fairies.

The Tailor sits in his corner, the master of circumstance and captain of his soul. If the roof fell in upon him he would but shake himself, and straightaway remember a case of similar occurrence and some curious story attached to the happening.

Ansty is direct and spontaneous in her thoughts and the expression of them. She uses the same earthy language to whomsoever she may be talking, regardless of their attitude, and she revels a little in the surprise and shock which she often produces. A twinkle comes to her eye at the least sign of your discomfiture. You do well to keep a poker face for Ansty. The Tailor adapts himself both in his speech and his subject matter to his listener, and in all ways endeavours to please.

'Listen to the to-o-one of him, will you?' interjects Ansty. 'You'd think it was to the Pope himself he was talking, he's so grand.'

Both are fluent Irish speakers. The Tailor is somewhat of an authority on the language, but has little patience with the hot-house cultivation or revival of the language, to which he refers with scorn as 'the boiling programme' (bi-lingual programme). They share a genius, too, for the coining and the use of strange words, which until you have become accustomed to them, are as a foreign language. They use them, play with them, and do not worship them. Seldom do they refer to anyone by their familiar names. Each has a nickname of their own invention, so that a conversation between them is often a series of riddles to an outsider.

The Tailor both reads and writes. Both of these arts are profound mysteries to Ansty, and she treats them with respect as though they were arts of the devil. On the occasion when the Tailor is stirred to correspondence, Ansty assists as Acolyte. The table is erected and carefully wiped. Ansty bears in, from the Room, the box containing the stationery, the pen and bottle of ink, and then sits silently and watches and waits.

The Tailor fishes out whatever flies have drowned themselves in the ink-bottle, and then braces himself for the job. First of all he must find the address of his correspondent. If that is not immediately forthcoming, it is always enough excuse for deferring the task until tomorrow.

He has been caught several times in some sort of trap, and has developed a deep suspicion of the whole postal service. After all his labours letters have been returned to him undelivered. He has grown wary now and usually gets someone else to address the envelopes, for his own version of addresses does not always comply with regulations. He is quite indifferent as to where he puts his own or his correspondent's. Sometimes his own will be on the envelope.

He tells the story about his own experience, when he was asked to write a letter by some woman to her brother in America. 'After spending a piece of the night at the job, I asked her for the address to which the letter was to be sent. "Oh, just address it to Micky Sullivan, Rocky Mountains, America!" said she.'

Occasionally the Tailor will deign to read the paper to Ansty. Again it is the mystery of the art which entrances her. The folds are pressed out of the paper. The Tailor puts on his spectacles; as a matter of form, not because his eyes need them. Ansty sits bolt upright, tense with attention. The Tailor chooses an account of the meeting of the County Council and begins.

'At Clonakilty, on the first of June –'

'Wisha!' exclaims Ansty, with a voice filled with wonder. 'At Clonakilty? ... Glory be! ... On the first of June? ... The Lord save us! ... That for 'oo!... On the first of June, at

Clonakilty!' She will continue to orchestrate on a couple of phrases and her exclamations and silence without paying any further attention to the content of the reading. Then suddenly the charm is broken. She will whirl up from the chair like a tornado, at the sound of a cart or footsteps on the road – and the ceremony is brought to an abrupt finish. Life is more important than news.

Ansty's world is very limited and personal. Bantry and Macroom come within the compass of it. Cork is a strain upon her imagination. Beyond Cork lies the rest of the world, and Heaven and Hell. When the labours of the day are ended she can still sit and listen to the Tailor talking with fresh wonder, though she must have heard most of it until she knows it by heart herself.

But only at night, by the fire, does she show this respect for him. During the day it is otherwise. The Tailor may be sitting, contentedly expounding some point or other, while perhaps the rain lashes down outside. Ansty comes in. She leans on her broom for a moment. The rain drips from her. Then she will interrupt him with contempt.

'Hmph! You – sitting there with your bottom in the ashes discussing 'feelosophy' and the rain slashin' in at the door!'

The Tailor simulates anger at the interruption.

'Thon amon dieu!' (T-anam an diabhal – your soul to the devil.) 'What would you have me do? Do you want me to sit with my bottom to the door to keep the rain out?'

For many, many years, Ansty has worn, on weekdays, the same clothes, until she has become, as the Tailor describes her, 'more like a blessed bush at a holy well than a woman', so tattered are her clothes. Yet the Tailor vows that she has a goodly stock of clothes upstairs – 'the grandest museum of clothes you ever did see. There'll be a great auction at her wake, for some of the dresses are so old that their like no longer exists in the world today. They are so old that they have been in and out of fashion twice already.'

On Sundays and holy days, however, Ansty surprises you. She combs up her Medusa-like hair, and puts on her black West Cork cloak with the hood thrust back. Then you realise that she was once the beauty of the neighbourhood, and beneath the filigree of wrinkles is still beautiful; still, in spite of the sharpness of her tongue, is delicate and feminine. Her eyes seem to regain the blue of the skies, and her hair, now tamed, you see is still golden amidst the silver. She is so changed that you might think her everyday self a pose, so that her Sunday self may always startle you.

Sunday is her high day. She goes to Mass and meets all the people she knows, and talks to them all in her racy manner. The Tailor stays at home and minds the house. All days are high days and holidays to him. 'Come day. Go day. Let's have another day.' But on Sundays, he changes his shirt and wears the black hat at a different angle.

All these comparisons are only comparisons of surfaces and appearances. Beneath all the seeming asperity of her appearance Ansty has a heart as big as the Tailor's. After the period of the rigour of her scrutiny and the shrewishness of her tongue, Ansty has an affection as great, a gratitude as deep, a kindliness as gentle as has the Tailor. Her home and all that she has and all that she can do for you are yours, gladly given, for Ansty and the Tailor, though they are two aspects of the same medal, are made of the same metal.

The whitewashed cottate of Garrynapeaka is, in outward appearance, much like all such cottages built under the Labourers' Cottage Act. It contains four rooms, two upstairs – the Loft – and two downstairs.

The heart of the place is the open fireplace with a black, sooty crane and the pot-hooks hanging from it, and the fire which never dies. At night the embers of the fire are smoored with ashes and in the morning are uncovered again and kindled into flame with chips of 'fir', the dried resinous wood from the bottom of the bogs.

The Tailor acts as Vesta. For years, until it has become a delicate art, he has tended and watched and nursed this heart of the house. He takes a great delight in astonishing you with his skill, and will let the fire die down until Ansty is almost speechless with wrath, and you, the spectator, imagine that at last the fire must be relit and the hearth desecrated with a match.

Slowly, so that you are the more impressed, the Tailor sets to work ... He rakes the last embers to the front. Methodically he builds a wall of sods of turf at the back and then feeds a few splinters of 'fir' and small pieces of turf to the faint embers and stacks more turf about them. A few subtle wafts from his hat, neither too gentle nor too vigorous, and presto! there is a lively leaping fire again and a twinkle in the tailor's eye at the sight of your wondering approbation.

Only once, some years ago when he discarded his cap for the Saint's soft black hat, did he almost fail. Almost but not quite. The ritual had been performed almost to the last. Only the wafting remained to be done. He took off the new black hat and fanned the pile with it. There was no response. He fanned harder, but it looked as though he was beaten.

Hurling the hat from him in disgust he seized the old cap again and the fire responded immediately.

'The divil mend it! Whatever powers a priest may have they are not in his hat.'

Since then he has developed the technique with the hat, and all is well.

By the side of the road there is a rick of turf for the fire and a pile of 'fir' for the kindling. All through the day the fire is busy, for all the cooking is done upon it and Ansty is always boiling water for tea or for the cow or for washing. In the winter, when the dark days come and the nights are long, there are logs to be burnt with a glow and a crackle, while the neighbours sit round and smoke, and the Tailor supplies them with entertainment far richer than money could buy.

At one side of the fire is an upturned butter-box. This is the Tailor's fireside seat. It is placed so that its opening is between his legs, and here he sits, never upon a chair.

Like everything else in the house it has a name. The Tailor refers to it always as 'Cornucopia' and explains that a long time ago a Greek king gave such a box to a 'jolly cupper', who gave him a drink when he was thirsty, telling her that whenever she was in the want of anything she had but to look inside and she would find it there.

'Glory be!' chimes Ansty. 'Anything she wanted! Ring a dora!'

'Yes, anything she wanted,' raps back the Tailor, 'but like all women she needed sense most of all but did not know it.'

For a moment Ansty is beaten, but immediately rallies.

'Did she look for a man in it?' she asks, with a leer.

'She did,' replies the Tailor. 'Didn't I tell you there was anything she wanted inside in it?'

'Aha!' laughs Ansty, 'that for 'oo! She found a man in it!' Then after a moment's silence, while her victory sinks in, her mood changes. 'The divil mend you! you don't fall into it yourself, the way you spend the day and the night with your backside glued to it, like an old statoo!'

To tell the strict truth, the Tailor does periodically fall into it. He estimates that a butter-box lasts him about three years and then collapses beneath him. But it is never changed until it fails. He enjoys the element of danger and surprise. Besides, it would break a ritual.

Whatever Amalthea's horn held, the Tailor's 'Cornucopia' almost rivals it for contents. Beneath the axe with the insecure head, with which he chops wood upon the hearthstone, and the goose-wing with which he sweeps up the ashes, there is a collection of bits of cloth, cords, tins, bits of tools and such-like things, out of which he can always find a makeshift for almost anything.

Across the hearth, opposite to this, is the chair of honour. Once upon a time it was a chair, but age and usage have worn down the legs unevenly till the seat of it is only a stool's height from the floor and its centre of gravity differs from that of all chairs. The back of it is loose and the brace of the back holds a bent and jagged piece of iron, held with four bent nails. To sit on it successfully, without being hurled to the floor, is a feat of no mean dexterity. To rise from it without a jag or a tear is almost a miracle. The Tailor always bows the most favoured guest to it as though it was a throne.

There are other chairs, strong chairs, sound chairs, even new chairs, about the house, but those are only for minor guests in the Tailor's order of precedence. If you visit him alone, perforce you sit in the chair of honour. Ladies, too, have this preference. Ansty sits there in the evenings and does not give way to locals. If several people are visiting, the order of precedence is arranged, with a masterly courtesy, by a wave of the hand and a word. Ansty wipes the seats of the other chairs with a definitely wet cloth and retires to the settle. Cornucopia is sacrosanct. No one ever violates it. Even Ansty, no matter how weary, would not dare to sit down. What would happen if she did there is no telling and no use in wondering. It would simply be akin to the sun not rising or black being white.

There are times, however, when the Tailor's diplomacy is swept aside by Ansty's more abrupt methods. If a guest should already be installed in the chair of honour and a guest of higher rank arrives, Ansty will simply and directly command, 'Get up, 'oo, and give the chair to So-and-so.'

Over the fireplace is 'the clevy', a shelf filled with tins. One contains sugar and another tea. There is a box of pepper and one containing caraway seeds, which Ansty mixes with tea. The remainder of the tins are mysteries. Never during any operation in the economy of the house are they opened. Never is their contents appealed to as an illustration. Perhaps they are but tins without contents and simply are, as the collection of dishes and plates on the dresser, awaiting an occasion still buried in the future.

In the middle of 'the clevy' is a cardboard box. That, too, has its mystery. It is a mystery, however, which has been revealed, or partly revealed. For it contains the clock, shut away from sight and dust, but whether it is a protection from sight or from dust is part of the mystery, for it is never consulted.

Behind 'Cornucopia', against the wall, is the settle. In the corner of this, directly behind the Tailor, is the Office. This is his accumulation of correspondence over the years. There are letters, photos, postcards from all over the world, stacked up into a pile. Here, too, is his box of cuttings from papers. There are paragraphs cut from newspapers relating to people he knows mixed up with accounts of freak calves and such-like wonders. Between the arm of the settle and the wall are his pipes. Each pipe, each letter and each photo recalls a friend.

Sometimes the Tailor will stretch himself at his ease on the settle. His head will rest in the Office, 'amongst his friends', and the correspondence will become a little more muddled after his repose than it was before, and the next time that he wants to show you a letter it will be more difficult to find it, 'but, what harm? There is always tomorrow.'

By the door as you come in stands the dresser with its stock of ware. Just as Cornucopia is the Tailor's preserve so is this Ansty's preserve. The Tailor never goes near it. Twice a year the settle and the dresser and the doors and the shutters of the windows are painted by Ansty until by now the accumulation of paint must be near to half an inch thick.

The Tailor never gives a hand, and views it all with cynical amusement. The only good that he can see in it is that it keeps the paint manufacturers busy and makes them rich. Ansty sees it in a very different light. It is a part of her round of worry. The house must be clean in case she should die tomorrow and the place not be ready for her wake. The Tailor's view is the more practical, for during the period of 'giving the place a rough dash', as he calls it, he has no peace. He is hounded from one place to another, and wherever he goes seems to be just the one place Ansty wants to paint or whitewash. Then he does seem to get a lot of the paint and the wash on to himself, too, before it ends and it looks as though he really did all the work.

Above the settle, on the wall, hang some religious pictures and the little red lamp of the Sacred Heart and the wall lamp for the night. The care of the lamps is one of the Tailor's duties. At about the same time each day he takes down the two lamps, unscrews them, refills them, and cleans the glass chimneys and replaces them for the night.

Beyond the kitchen is The Room. Ansty speaks of it always in capital letters. The Tailor, however, refers to it as his studio. It does at least contain the tools of his trade. There is the sewing machine, which has not been used for years. Never since the day when he took some part out of it, and Ansty lost it before he had time to replace it, and the Tailor took that as a sign that the days of his serious work were over. There is also a pressing-board and a goose-iron and a collection of patterns of cloth.

Ansty makes more use of the Room. Here she keeps her pans of milk for cream and the churn for the butter-making. There is, too, a collection of the years, of odds and ends. The Tailor is little interested in the place and very seldom goes into it. It is a museum of the past, and the reality of the past lies in his own mind and not in mere things.

Upstairs are the bedroom, with a great box-bed, and the small room beyond where Ansty keeps the meal and corn so that even at night when she is asleep she can still guard it from the pilfering of the rats and the mice.

The whitewashed cottage, which is a landmark from the hills about, stands in an acre of thin-soiled, mountainy land. It is set with potatoes and a little hay and oats and cabbage. In the middle of it tower two huge ivy-covered rocks which provide a vantage-point for the Tailor when he is 'minding the dairy herd', and for the more practically minded Ansty, make an excellent place for the drying and the bleaching of her wash.

Neighbours give them help with the small labour of ploughing and digging and reaping, and come gladly. A day with the Tailor is reward enough. No one passes the road without paying a call. Very seldom does a night pass, summer or winter, that some one at least, and more often several, do not drop in for the nightly 'scoruiocht' at the Tailor's.

They are known and loved for miles around. Wherever you go in West Muskerry you hear 'The Tailor and Ansty! They're an airy couple!'

The Tailor is a gentleman of leisure. He stays in bed each morning until 'Sean the Post' arrives on his way up from the village, with whatever letters there may be, and the much more important local news he may have collected on his four miles journey from the village.

But, as the Tailor says, he gets paid for simply being alive, sleeping or waking, in the form of his ten shillings a week pension, and he will not get any more by getting up any earlier. The rest of the people can air the world for him and put it straight before he gets up.

Ansty is full of busyness. She gets up with the dawn, kindles the fire, makes tea, lets out the cow, and from this until evening is always on the go. Though the Tailor may view much of her activity with scorn, someone must do the work of the place. The soda bread must be baked, the clothes washed, turf and water have to be carried, the cow and the hens and the ducks have to be fed, and in between, so that there will be no idle moment, the floor must be swept and swept and swept.

'Did you ever know how dust came to be invented?' asks the Tailor, after he has been disturbed innumerable times. 'Well, I'll tell you the reason. When God made women they straightaway got into mischief. You see, He forgot to give them any sort of brains, and it was too late to do anything about it then. So He had an idea. He invented dust so that they should be all day sweeping it from one end of the house to the other. But it wasn't a great success. They still manage to get into mischief.'

The Tailor does, however, play a part in the ritual of Garrynapeaka beyond that of critic. He tends the fire and cooks the dinner. He digs the potatoes and washes them and boils them. He prepares the meat. Then he tends and fills the lamps. Each day he has a round of duties and each day of the week there is some extra duty, particular to the day, added to his none too onerous burden.

On Wednesdays he 'makes the churn', which is strenuous work for even a strong man. The churn is an old-fashioned dash churn, seldom seen nowadays, and the churn is 'made' by working a plunger up and down in it until the cream 'cracks' and the butter forms.

Sitting on Cornucopia, he twists his withered leg round the top of the little barrel and 'slashes away', now and again pausing to sing a snatch of a song which has come into his mind. Then he salts the butter and that is Wednesday's labour finished.

Another day in the week you may come to the half-door and find him sitting before a tub and a basket, washing the eggs to fulfil the requirements of some Sale of Eggs Act. Of course, as soon as anyone appears the eggs are forgotten and all the evils of washing them remembered.

'Washing eggs! God blast it! Did you ever hear the like?' he says, as though he had been caught red-handed committing a crime. 'As though people haven't eaten eggs for thousands of years without washing them until these politicians came along with their nonsensical notions. I tell you there's no face to it. One of these days the same politicians will come along and teach the hens how to lay them. It is a strange but a true thing, that the worse the Government the more Acts of Parliament they pass. I remember the days ...' and so the Tailor's interest moves far away from his work on the eggs and his interest in them and he regains his seat on Cornucopia.

A shadow falls across the half-door.

'Thon amon dieul! I suppose you're tired,' says the voice of Ansty with bitter sarcasm, 'or the box in the corner was getting cold without your backside on top of it and the eggs can wait.'

'By the mockstick of war!' replies the Tailor, 'you'd think to listen to you that the whole country was crying out for eggs, and you were the only one who had them. They can wait till tomorrow,' he adds with decision. 'There'll likely enough be another Act of Parliament passed today whereby you'll be transported for washing eggs at all.' And that day's labour is ended, at least, to the Tailor's satisfaction.

Each day has its round of general and particular duties, but the culmination of the week, the Tailor's most strenuous day, is Saturday.

The midday meal is finished. The Tailor has fed the cat and the dog. He has replaced the black hat upon his head and turned to the fire and is busy in the effort of getting his pipe to draw.

Ansty asks, 'Have you cleaned the knives and the forks yet? Are you going to sit there for the rest of the day without stirring?'

'Maybe I will,' answers the Tailor placidly between the

puffs and the pulls. 'I'm beginning to get a liking for the seat.'

Ansty whirls out in disgust to attend to ducks or hens or the cow, and the Tailor continues to puff and to pull.

Soon, however, Ansty returns to the charge.

'Knives and forks! Knives and forks!' snorts the Tailor after listening to her for a moment. 'Is the Pope coming to tea or what the hell ails you with your "knives and forks"?'

About three o'clock he stirs himself and does get the box of knives and forks. There are about a dozen of each. They have never been used and are never likely to be used. They are of the company of the many dishes on the dresser and the many tins on 'the clevy'. They are ciphers in the life of Garrynapeaka, meaning nothing in themselves, as the noughts in a million, but just as important.

Out of Cornucopia the Tailor produces a knifeboard, some brick-dust and a polishing rag, and with much puffing and blowing he polishes them. The man who made them originally used far less effort in the making of them than the Tailor does in the needless cleaning of them.

Having by now got the flavour of stirring himself, he proceeds to his weekly shave. He takes water out of the kettle, which Ansty always wants for some other purpose. Out of Cornucopia again comes a small mirror and a shaving-brush and razor. The razor is one given to him forty years ago by a friend in the old Royal Irish Constabulary. For forty years it was neither ground nor set, and was used for many purposes other than shaving. Shaving with it must have been either a magical process or a form of hell.

But those days are over. A friend took it over to London and had it ground and set in St James' Street. After the first shave with it the Tailor said that his face did not know the rest of his body and they had to be introduced to each other again. At last the shaving is finished. Life is arduous.

This is the one occasion in the week when he really feels in need of the refreshment of a cup of tea, and he puts the kettle hanging on the fire as soon as the shaving is finished. During the rest of the week he is indifferent to it. It is Ansty who hangs the kettle and is always ready for tea.

Down comes a contraption from the settle. It is a collapsible table with a hanging leg. One end rests on the settle and the other is supported by the swinging leg. It is just the right height for the Tailor seated on Cornucopia and the wrong height for anyone sitting on a chair. The Tailor is proud of this and enjoys your interest.

'What is it? Yerra, manalive!' he says, giving it a resounding thump, 'that's a table. You've never seen the likes of that before I'll bet for a wager, yet that has been in this world for the past six hundred years, and you'd get a better meal off that than off any table de hote in the world.'

'Have a cup?' asks Ansty, with a lively interest.

'Will 'oo have "colouring"?' she asks then.

'Colouring' is Ansty's term for milk. She will present you with a really excellent cup of tea, far better than you will get in most hotels. The Tailor will ask you to have a cut of soda cake, or he will toast a slice of baker's bread for you. Ansty will ask you to have a boiled egg.

The Tailor will abide by your decision. Ansty will continue to persuade you, until a minor war breaks out between them and you, and the tea, and Ansty's hostess manners are all forgotten as they wrangle together. Suddenly the war ends as it started. Ansty hears someone passing and in the middle of the sentence leaps up, 'Hould!' and rushes to the half-door to see who is passing, for all who pass must stand her scrutiny.

If they come into the yard she will speak to them over the half-door and you may hear your hostess in another manner.

'Have a "heat of the tea"?' she invites.

The answer is always a refusal from those who know her.

'Scratch your bottom, then,' is her answer, and she returns to the table to pick at a piece of bread like a bird.

Another duty of the day in which the Tailor is involved is that of winding the clock. Each evening, at about the same time, Ansty will break in upon his talk.

'Did you wind the clock?'

'I did not,' replies the Tailor automatically.

'Better do it and then talk.'

The cardboard box in the middle of 'the clevy' is opened and a stout alarm-clock is taken out. It is given exactly the same number of turns of the key each night and replaced in the box and the lid of the box closed until the same performance the following evening. It is never consulted. No attention is paid to see whether it is right or wrong. The Tailor has some sort of a notion that it is a day wrong, but he is not sure whether it is a day fast or a day late. He is not interested in clock time.

'The best clock any man ever had is his belly. That tells him when it is time to eat. And when there is no one sitting by the fireside, then it's time to go to bed. And the time to get up is when you are tired of being in bed.'

The Tailor is not interested in the clock. Ansty cannot read it. You wonder sometimes if maybe this clock, so carefully guarded in 'the clevy' in Garrynapeaka, has more than ordinary importance, and if it may not be the clock of the universe, and if Ansty forgot to remind the Tailor to wind it, tomorrow the sun might fail to rise.

Along with the clock, each evening the Tailor has to be reminded to close and secure the outhouses. Ansty will wait, with malice aforethought, for an opportune moment to prick the bubble of his eloquence and rouse him to a sense of forgotten duty.

On one such occasion, his pipe drawing well, he was retailing the history of a former local resident, a General Gatacre, whose chief claim to fame, in the Tailor's estimation, was the fact that he once shot and ate one of the swans on the lakes nearby. He was sailing gaily into the subject, which held all sorts of possibility of extension. Ansty, leaning on her broom by the door, waited until he had almost reached the climax of his story. Then her voice broke in.

'Go out and shut up the ducks,' she commanded, 'and close the fowls' house, and fasten the Room's window, and settle the door of the stall, and ... you-can-come-in-and-sit-on-your-backside-for-the-rest-of-the-evening-and-talk-about ... General Gatacre!'

The scorn with which she said 'General Gatacre', as

93

though the Tailor was far beyond his depth, defeated the Tailor utterly. He went out and did her bidding, and no one ever heard the end of the story of General Gatacre and the swan.

A duty which the Tailor does treat with respect is that of 'standing to the cow'. This consists of watching every movement of the black cow, exhorting it, checking it, shouting at it, getting Carlo to bark at it, building impregnable barriers between it and the oats and the cabbage and the potatoes.

In Ansty's scheme of things this cow comes first, and it is capable of every form of devilment that ever flickered through a cow's mind. If it is not guarded, it is liable to every misfortune that can possibly happen to a cow. Ansty, by the vehemence of her faith, seems to have won the Tailor to the same faith, and he grumbles only occasionally at this service to 'the hub of the household'. Only when at last the cow is shut up for the night in its warm and clean thatched stall does peace of any kind light upon Garrynapeaka.

The day ends with the last duty of all of the Tailor. At the end of the day, by the fireside, he and Ansty say the Rosary together in Irish. All the differences of the day are ended and forgotten, and the meaningless curses and the quarrels of habit and the rough, unvarnished words are solved, and banished with the prayers of the Rosary.

The weather and the day's news had been discussed and dismissed.

'I was telling you the other day,' started the Tailor, 'of the way they had in the old days for managing clothes. But the world had changed a lot since then and a lot of the things they did and the ways they had have gone like the snow on Mangerton last year.

'Have you ever seen Mangerton mountain? It is one of the highest mountains in Kerry, and I know it well. You may be sure that I do, for I was born and reared within sight of it.

'My father was a farmer of twenty-four "collops", in the parish of Kilgarvin, in the county of Kerry, and I was born there in 1862. Maybe you have not heard tell of "collops". It's a knowledge that is dying out of the world.

'Well, collops was the old style of reckoning for land, before the people got too bloodyful smart and educated, and let the Government or anyone else do their thinking for them. A collop was the old count for the carrying power of land. The grazing of one cow or two yearling heifers or six sheep or twelve goats or six geese and a gander was one collop. The grazing for a horse was three collops.

'I tell you, that was a better style of reckoning than your acres and your yards. It told you the value of a farm, not the size of it. An acre might be an acre of rock, but you know where you are with a collop. There is a man over there on the other side of the valley has four thousand acres of land, and barely enough real land to graze four cows in the whole lot. But you would think he had a grand farm when you talk of acres. The devil be from me! but the people in the old days had sense.

'There were thirteen of us in family, and I was the seventh son of my father, who was the seventh son of his father, so that the natural strain of a doctor is in me. I don't mean one of those galoots who have the title of being doctor but have no knowledge, but the type of doctor who has the knowledge within him and to hell with the title. Because a man has read a book does not mean that he is a wise man. There is too much learning in books nowadays, and too little learning in the head.

'We lived hard in those days. There was no tea and no bread and no sugar. I remember the first tea that came and how they made it. Some man who had been into Cork brought tea home as a great wonder, and had all the talk of what it would be. Well, his wife made a hand of it, and the way she had was to boil it and to strain off the water, and they fell to, eating the leaves as though it was cabbage. I saw that happen with my two eyes, as sure as there's a tail on a cat.

'We lived hard and we lived on the product of the land, on oatmeal, potatoes and milk. Probably we would kill an old cow or a couple of goats for Christmas, and that was all the meat we had for the year.

'When spring would come there would be as much

95

potatoes as would do us until May. They usen't to set potatoes until July, and it is how they used to set them was to graff the scalp off the land with mattocks, and then when that dried, they burned it and shook the ashes on the ground. That was the manure they had.

'Then they would turn that into ridges with spades, for they had no ploughs, and they set the seed in the ground then and earthed it. They had fine potatoes called Black Minions. There are no such potatoes nowadays.

'It was in 1881 that the Champions first came to Ireland from Scotland, after the failure of 1880. They were allotted by the Board of Guardians. The law was that you would get so many hundred according to your valuation, and they should be paid for out of the poor rate. Poor people that had no land, but were workmen to farmers, would get two hundred by getting two securities.

'There was a man by the name of Dan Gill, who lived in Fussa. He had his two securities got and signed, and he went to Kenmare for three days, and it was failing him to get his potatoes because all the world was there. On the third day he got to the door of the courthouse, after a struggle, to where the committee was, and he made application to them.

'"You gentlemen before me are selected for the upkeep of the county and the welfare of the people, and I hope that you are conscientious men and do not make a zig-zag of your conscience, and that you understand the difference between God and Tom Bell (who is the devil's father), and that you will deal fairly with me, who am an old man, seventy-two years of age, and this is my third day walking twelve miles, six miles in and six miles out."

'I took great admiration for this when I heard it. It was as fine and as good an oration as ever I heard.

'But to get back to the way we had of living in my young days. Before the potatoes would be ripe they would cut the corn. They would burn the top of the sheaf of oats, and that would harden the oats for the quern, for the quern was how they used to grind the oats.

'The quern was a fake made with two flat stones, one on top of the other. You would put the oats between the two and turn the top one with a bit of a stick, and the oats between would be crushed. When the oats was ground in the quern, they would put the chaff and the shell into a tub, and put water on that, and leave it rest until tomorrow. That would lift all the chaff to the top. Tomorrow they'd throw that off, and what remained behind was "flimmery". They would put cold water on that for three days, and on the third night they would boil it, and it was the grand meal.

'They used to make a kind of bread with potatoes called "Stampy". They would grate the potatoes on a tin grater, and then squeeze them into a tub of water. From the water they would get the starch for the clothes. There was no such thing as a bastable in those days. The "Stampy" was made on a breadtree, which was a kind of sloping board put before the fire to hold the bread, as you would make toast nowadays. "Stampy" was usually only made for Christmas or November Night, unless you had a good supply of potatoes, when you might make it once a week.

'On the first of May the people would remove to the mountains, and make a bit of a house against a rock with sticks and scraws. They would carry their cattle, their milking cattle, with them, and milk them, and make butter and pack firkins, and send them to Cork by the carriers.

'When they were out of potatoes, they used to live on so many pints of blood out of the cow. First of all they would pull the rushes, and then pull the heart out of them and put it crosswise into a pot, and put the blood on to that. About halfways again they would put another crossing of rushes and then more blood, and then they would boil the blood until it was hard like a cake, and that was what they would have for food.

'They would make curds, too, of sour milk, and mix goats' milk through it. They would leave the whey run out of the door, and it would run out through the land. When November came, there would be a green stream of grass from the door, and they would measure this. By the length of this green stream the wealth of a man was measured. The man with the longest stream was the man who had the best times.

97

'They were hard ways of living then. Those were the days of the evictions and the Land League and the Coercion Acts. I remember, when Balfour's Coercion Act came out, a man described it this way:

*You'll have to tell the hour that you were born,*
*And the way that you were got,*
*And the hour that you were made,*
*And how your mother met the man.*

'That struck me as a very witty piece of business when I heard it.

'The people of this country were badly and unjustly treated, and that made the hardship of their lives the more. I don't blame the English people for this. It was the English Government, and you can't judge a people by its Government. I know that the English people had to suffer the same Government, and Governments are never made of the best of a people.

'But the English Government made a rod for their own backs. Did you know that the great Boer General, De Wet, who beat the English in the Boers' War, was of Irish descent? His father was an Irishman. I'll tell you the whole story.

'General De Wet's father was from Laune, west of Killarney. He was O'Connor, one of the O'Connor Balcarres, good, stout blocks of men. He was transported from Ireland to Algery on the west coast of Africa. They call it "the white man's grave". He was transported for smuggling tobacco, which was a custom they had in those days, and the devil a bit of harm was there in it. They did harm to no man.

'Well, enough, begod, he was landed in Algery, and he was put in a camp, and it wasn't agreeing with him at all. It wasn't long before he got away from them and went on the run. He faced up a mountain, and soon they had to give him up. He was too much for them, for he was a terrible loose type of a man, and mountains were nothing at all to him.

'Come the following morning, he faced down the other side of the mountain, and he hadn't gone very far at all when he came across some people, and they were all black.

He had never seen the like before and they had never seen the like of him before; but being a decent, civil type of man he spoke to them.

'He had no English, but only the Irish, and to each man he met he said, "Dia Dhuit" (Good day). That was his salute.

'By the hokey! when they saw him, never having seen the likes of him before, a white man, they thought that he was God, come down from Heaven, and they adored him and took him up and gave him the hell of a good time. He said to himself that this was better than the transportation camp, and he might as well die in June as July, so he anchored there.

'They called him De Wet, which was as near as they could get to the Irish, thinking it was his name. Anyway, after some time he got into a share of their ways, and they came to an understanding and he became a great man amongst them. Well, the devil a bit, but after a while longer he became intimate with one of the black women, and they got married, and they had a son, and that son was De Wet, General De Wet.

'I tell you that it was then the English Government began to learn that they had only done themselves a great harm, when they thought that they were doing themselves a great good, by transporting O'Connor to Algery, thinking they had heard the last of him in "the white man's grave".

'They were hard times and they were difficult times, but there was plenty of fun. There were weddings and wakes and all sorts of amusements that the people made themselves.

'The people were very interested in dancing in those days, and there were dancing masters. They used to make a little hut, and you would carry a bag of turf tonight that would do the fire, and I would carry one tomorrow night. That was the payment. There were no such thing as "sets". There was only step-dancing, jigs and reels – no more.

'For music they had fiddles and flutes. There were no melodeons then. Sometimes there was not even fiddle and flute. Then they would dance to "puss-music", music made by the mouth alone, without any instrument. I remember to

99

see the first bagpipes made by some fellows, north in Ballyvourney, who made them from sheepskins and reeds and their own ingenuity, and a queer kind of music it sounded then.

'There was a dancing master in my time, by the name of Moriarty, who had an awkward block of a fellow to teach. It was failing Moriarty altogether to teach him how to batter, so, begod, he got a gad and put it on his left leg, and a sugan (hay rope) on the right, and he caught the ends of them in his two hands, and while the music was playing Moriarty sang this song.

> *Rise upon Sugan,*
> *Sink upon Gad.*
> *Shuffle, me lad,*
> *Both Sugan and Gad.*

'I tell you that he soon made a smart dancer of him.

'Hurley ball was the sport of my time. They made hurleys out of ash sticks, and a ball out of homespun thread from old stockings, covered with a leather covering. That was a terrible fierce game. There was no referee. There was no such thing as rules. It was a right murderers' game, but they were tough, strong men in those days, and they would think nothing at all of a blow which would kill a man nowadays.

'Tobacco was cheap, and porter was cheap, and whiskey was cheap, and a man could get a deal of pleasure that way at little cost. The people, too, were a wittier, more airy people altogether. There was more talk, and good talk. There would never be a "Scoruiocht" without some grand fun and songs and stories. The people had their own amusements. They had no need to seek other amusements.

'But that is all over now, like the fair of Athy, and the wise man is he who makes the best of what is, and remembers what was. I hear herself coming. I'd better look busy.'

The rain was slashing down outside. All the Tailor's duties had been performed. Ansty had at last settled down and there was a merry fire on the hearth.

'Did you ever hear tell of a class of fellows called "the cabogues"?' asked the Tailor, as the prelude to a story. 'Well, I'll tell you a story about two of them, and what happened to them.

'In years gone by it was ever a custom of fellows from Castletown and Allihies and such-like places to go down to Limerick, to dig spuds for the farmers in the autumn. They were known as cahogues. They would start off on a Saturday morning with a spade and a shirt, and go to Mallow that night, no matter what the distance. The following day, Sunday, after Mass, the farmers would be looking for the men for hiring.

'Well, there were two young recruits to the game. They would be about eighteen years of age, and it was their first time going on the expedition. They set out good and early, and that night they reached Mallow. They had never been in the likes of the town of Mallow before, and they knew no one there.

'They did not know where they would sleep that night, so they asked a man they met in the street, and he took them to a lodging-house and told them to anchor there. They had the supper, and when the time came for them to go to bed they were surprised where they were going, when the landlady showed them the way upstairs.

'This was a great wonder to them, for at that time in the country there was no upstairs nor loft to any house. Just a room here and another one off it, all on the level.

'There were two beds in the room. They were told to sleep there, but one bed would do them, they said, as they always slept together.

'Well, begod, the landlady walked down from them, and as soon as she was gone they set to, and looked round the room and examined everything in it, for it was all strange to them. There was in it all manner of things, the like of which they had never set eyes on before. They came to the beds. They examined the fine linen on them and the frames of them. Then one of them looked underneath and he found a pot.

'"That's a queer article," said he, pulling it out.

101

'"It is," said the other fellow, pulling out the pot from under the other bed, and studying it. "What can they be for, I wonder?"

'"The devil alone knows," said his companion. "Could they be the tea-cups of Finn MacCool?"

'"Not at all," said the other fellow, who did not want to appear ignorant. "I'll tell you what they are. They are night-caps, of course."

'So they put on their night-caps and into bed with them, and they slept very comfortably entirely. At that time a four-horse coach left Mallow for Newcastle West at six o'clock in the morning. They used to call it a Jingle by the noise of the bells on the harness.

'Well, the devil a bit but the following morning my two jolly cuppers were wakened by the noise of the Jingle under the window, and they wondered what it could be. Out of the bed with them, and they stuck their heads outside the window to solve the mystery.

'The night-caps fell off into the street below and broke with the hell of a noise, which frightened the horses, and away with the Jingle and the grooms chasing it and shouting, and the passengers screeching, and everybody in Mallow thinking, with all the noise and clatter, that surely the last day had come. But it was all due to two cabogues who did not know the difference between a pot and a night-cap.

'But that was not the end of the expedition. The two cabogues were hired in Mallow that day, and went out to the potato digging. They earned good money, and at last the season was over, and they had to be taking the road for home again.

'Their route took them by way of Tipperary, and as they were passing along a road they came to a notice which said that for the payment of half a crown anybody could look at the Ratschilds' money.

'Now the Ratschilds were the richest people in the whole world, and the head of them lived in Tipperary. (I'll tell you afterwards how they came to get the money and the name). It was a custom of the head of them to let people see the wonder of money that they had, and to charge them for the sight of it, as the notice said.

'Said one cabogue to the other when they had the notice read, "I'm thinking that I'll take a look at that."

'"Thamwirrashimfaina!" said the other to him, "have you gone clean mad, to be paying half a crown to see another man's money? Have sense, man."

'"I have sense enough," replied the other. "It is seldom that the chance will come our way to be able to see such a wealth of money as the Ratschilds' money."

'"Go your way, then," said the sensible fellow, sitting on the bank of the road and lighting his pipe. "I will wait here for you."

'So, in with the first cabogue to the house, and he knocked on the door. The head of the Ratschilds opened it to him.

'"Good day," said the cabogue. "I have come to see your money."

'"That will cost you half a crown," said the Ratschild.

'So my jolly cupper handed him the half a crown, and the head of the Ratschilds took him into the room where the money was. In one corner was a heap of gold. In another a heap of silver, and in another a heap of coppers. The cabogue looked at it in wonder, for never before had he seen so much money in one place.

'"Well," said the Ratschild, after a few moments, "aren't you the foolish man to be paying me half a crown to look at my money?"

'"Yerra, not at all," replied the cabogue. "Doesn't the sight of it give me as much pleasure as it does you?"

'"True for you," replied the Ratschild, scratching his chin. "I suppose that it does. You are a smarter fellow than I thought," he went on, "for you have taught me, the richest man in the world, a lesson."

'"Ah! say no more about it," said the cabogue.

'"No," answered the head of the Ratschilds, "you deserve a reward. Help yourself."

'So the cabogue took up a fistful of gold and a fistful of silver, and out with him to the other fellow outside, who

103

was still smoking his pipe.

'"Now," said he, showing him the money, "am I the foolish fellow or are you?"

'"The devil fire you," said the other fellow, "you are a smarter fellow than I thought."

'"That is exactly what the Ratschild said to me," said the fellow with the money, "but he paid me for the lesson I taught him, but we will say no more about it."

'They went on their way and they came to a pub, and they went in and called for two half-gallons of porter, and drove the devil of a spree together.

'I suppose that you have heard of the Ratschilds and now they are the richest family in the world; but I bet for a wager you don't know how they came to be so wealthy, and how they came by the name.

'They started in Cork. Ratschild isn't their right name at all. They are really Kellihers, but they changed that. They used to be house painters in the beginning, and one day one of the brothers was painting a house, and he was on the scaffold having a smoke for himself, when he saw a rat come out of a hole, and it had a sovereign in its mouth.

'Rats are curious animals. They are very fond of collecting bright things and carrying them away to their nests. Well, this man by the name of Kelliher, went on quietly smoking and thinking to himself that house painting was a poor sort of life, and how he wished he had enough money to start some other kind of business, when he saw the rat come out again, and it had another sovereign. It placed this with the other and went back.

'Kelliher went on smoking and did nothing to frighten the rat, and the rat went on carrying out sovereigns and making a pile of them. When at last he had made a good pile, Kelliher threw his paint-brush at it, and came down from the scaffold, and collected up the pile of sovereigns and counted them, and found that he had come into the way of being a rich man.

'That was the beginning of the Ratschilds. They discontinued the house painting business and started a bank and soon were in a mighty way of business, and because they

104

had made their beginning from the money the rat had collected, they were ever afterwards called the Ratschilds, and the devil blast the lie it is.

'It is a queer thing the way fortunes are made, and how men come to be rich. It is seldom by hard work. Hard work chiefly kills a man. Did you ever hear the story of Laddin, and the curious thing that Laddin found, and the wonders that it would do?

'It all happened in Paris, which is the capital of France, except some part of it which happened in a big meadow in South Africa. It happened a long time ago, for I heard it told by an old man when I was a boy, and he was a young man when it happened.

'One day there was a party of young fellows playing a game of handball in the main streeet of the city of Paris. There was one fellow amongst them whose name was Laddin, and whose father was a tailor who was dead.

'A man, by the name of Musapha, came up to this young fellow and asked him was he Laddin.

'"Yes," said he, "the devil a wonder but I'd be Laddin. Wasn't I christened Laddin?"

'"Well," said Musapha, "will you come for a walk?"

'"I will,"' said Laddin, '"but I would like to tell my mother first."

'"Ah! To hell with your mother!" said Musapha then, "we won't be long away."

'"All right then," consented Laddin.

'They struck out of the town about three miles at their ease, and they went into the corner of a wood. Laddin was getting scared, but at the same time he took it softly and made the best of it. There was a small patch at the end of the wood where there was no grass growing, and Musapha put a ring on Laddin's small finger and told him to work with that finger in the ground.

'So Laddin did as he was told, and the devil a bit but he had only little done, when the place opened, and down he went with the devil's own landing, and the place overhead closed.

'"By the hokey!" said Laddin then, "I'm in the hell of a

105

fix."

'He shouted and called away, but no one answered him, and he was thinking that he would never again get up. But soon he came to steps, and trying to climb up them, and in the act of climbing up them in the dark, for there was ne'er a splink of light, he struck the ring against the steps and the ring asked what did he want.

'"Yerra, manalive," said Laddin, "what do you think I'd want but to get out of this place. Do you think that I am screeching for the fun of the thing?"

'The ring told him to go to a crevice in the cave and there he would find a lamp, and to bring the lamp with him.

'"Talk sense, man," said Laddin. "How can I find a lamp in a crevice when I cannot see my own hand?"

'The ring then told him to calm himself and to make search. Well, he made search, thinking that he might as well do that as any other thing, and he found the lamp. When he was above ground again Musapha was there, and Laddin gave him a relement.

'"The devil break your legs, didn't you hear me calling to you? It is a queer kind of fun to watch me fall into a bog hole and give me no help."

'When Laddin had finished, Musapha told him to keep the lamp carefully, and anything he wanted it would do him, to put his thumb into his mouth, and chew it and then tell the lamp, and the lamp would tell him what to do.

'He thanked Musapha and told him that he was grateful to him, but Musapha said, "Not at all. Damn it, it was nothing entirely."

'They walked the three miles back into the city, and there they parted and Laddin went home. His mother asked him were he had been, and why he was late for the tea, but he told her nothing at all. He went to bed after he had something to eat, for he was tired after the day's expedition, and he took the lamp with him and put it in a safe place under the bed.

'When he got up the following morning his mother said to him that there was nothing for the breakfast, for they were very poor. He thought of what Musapha had told him, and he went to the room above again and took out the lamp from under the bed, and put his thumb in his mouth and chewed it and told the lamp the trouble.

'The lamp talked and told him, "You make chinaware and take it out and sell it." So he took the lamp down over a table and struck it and told it to make chinaware. Down came a cup and saucer of chinaware. It was the prettiest piece of business ever a man did see. He made a dozen of each and took them out to the neighbours and sold them, and then they had the fine breakfast.

'After they had the breakfast finished he made some more, and put them in the window. The news got around, and the world got surprised, and the people came in troops, buying, and he selling, and all the time the grand ware was rattling on to the table as fast as he could sell it. Then he told it to make dishes and so on, and the lamp went obstreperous and there was no stopping it at all, and chinaware was pouring over the room and out into the street, and he came up to make a terrible big fortune.

'After a while the lamp got tired and stopped, and Laddin himself took a rest and got married. When he was married he no longer had time for the hardware busines, so he put the lamp under the bed again, where only he and his wife slept, and he told no one.

'One day he went out for a walk by himself, and some fellow in the city, who had been watching his movements, bought fine, grand, new lamps, and went round the houses calling, "New lamps for old!" He came to Laddin's house and walked in to his wife, and asked her for any old lamp she might have, and he would give her a fine new lamp for it.

'She remembered that one day when she was dusting and poking about she had come across the old lamp under the bed and, with the height of madness, she went upstairs and brought down the old lamp and gave it to him. He fulfilled his part of the bargain and then skedooed off. He asked the lamp where they should go, and the lamp told him to South Africa, so there they spent the night.

'When Laddin came home from his walk, his wife told

him of her bit of business, and showed him the grand new lamp and asked him if it was not the fine bargain.

'"Thon amon dieu!" exclaimed Laddin, "we are done for ever."

'"But, sure," said she, "wasn't it thrown idle?"

'"Idle me foot! That's the worst of the senselessness and the interference of women! If you would but attend to the business of the house, and not the things which do not concern you, all would have been well. We are ruined and disgraced."

'He would eat no dinner. Away with him saying that he would travel the world for ever till he found the man who had stolen the lamp; and then it would go hard with him. So he travelled for four days and for four nights, and the fourth night he slept under a hedge.

'When he woke he went to a stream to wash his face, and in the act of taking up water to his face he struck the ring upon a rock and the ring asked him what ailed him, and whyfor was he travelling the world.

'"What ails me? Why am I travelling the world? Aren't those foolish questions! What the devil do you think ails me? Do you think that I am travelling the world for the good of my health?"'

'"Aisy now, aisy," said the ring. "I'll tell you all that you want to know if you but listen."

'Then the ring told him that the man who had stolen his lamp was in the middle of a big meadow in South Africa, and was in the act of enjoying the finest breakfast ever a man did see, provided by the power of the lamp.

'At that Laddin said that himself should go to South Africa, and with that he set off, and he never stopped until he got there, and he found the man just finishing his breakfast and the lamp beside him. He had a few words with him and took the lamp from him and by the power of it he changed the man into a stone statue so that he should steal no more lamps. When he had this done he sat down and finished the breakfast, there were lashings of the finest food.

'Then he felt better and returned to Paris with the lamp, leaving the man in the field to this day. He started again in

108

the hardware business, but no longer sought his conjugal
rights with his wife, but left well alone and lived happily.'

# After Hours

## Eamon Kelly*

Well, there was this public house I knew of a time. You'd hardly ever see anyone going into it or coming out of it. It was run by three sisters, fairly ancient, I'd say they were behind the door when the good looks were being given out. You'd want to be paid if you were to give any time looking at 'em. One of the sisters'd always be at the entrance, dyddling away for herself, looking up and down the street, the two hands under the apron. By the way, do you see, that it was a gay house.

The time the railways and the roads were cut during the second trouble there was an awful shortage of drink in town, and Ned Connor, when all fruit fails welcome haws, went into the public house I'm talking about. Ned had an awful mind for porter, he'd drink it out of a horse's crupper. The sister that was at the door dyddling the blackbird backed in before him.

Ned called for a pint, and when after a lot of taoscing she put it on the counter, Ned said, 'This pint isn't full.'

'Ah', says she, 'I left room on top for your moustache.'

Ned had what can only be described as a big straggly growth on the top lip. When he put up the money she found she was a few ha'pence short. The price of the moustache Ned told her. The porter was so flat, little súilíns winking on top of it, that it gave Ned enough to do to finish the pint.

When finally he got it down Ned made a move to go, and as she dyddled she kept an eye on him.

'Are you off?' she said.

'Oh I am,' says Ned.

'Of course,' says she, turning as sour as the commodity she was selling, 'only for the shortage of drink in town you wouldn't come into me at all.'

* From *In My Father's Time* by Eamon Kelly.

'Well I can tell you one thing,' says Ned, 'you'll have a lot of dyddling done before I'll come into you again!'

Ned was noted, but fierce, for the drink. He took every known pledge in his time including the anti-treating pledge. That was brought in to counteract the habit of standing your round, which is all right if the company is small, but if you have seven or eight in a batch, and maybe, before you know where you are, the man that opened the proceedings is off on the second leg of the course, then there's rough weather ahead. And the man of limited capacity don't he suffer! His wife at home thinking he is enjoying himself.

One of the pledges Ned took only allowed him one drink a day. He settled for a pint. That was all right until he was seen pouring two pints into a quart jug, making one drink of it. He went from the quart to the sweet gallon and finished up worse than ever. And I'll never forget one Whitsun I was going doing the rounds at Gobnet's Well, John Lynch was with me the same day and we got up to Ned going down Sliabh Riabhach.

Whit was late that year and it was very warm so we went into The Mills. I called and when the pints were put on the counter Ned Connor caught his glass and ran out in the yard with it. When he came back 'twas empty. John Lynch called then, and the same thing happened. Ned came back with the empty glass in his hand. 'Twas his own turn to call then and when he was making for the back door with the third pint 'twas only natural that myself or John Lynch'd remark on it. Well, for one thing he was playing poo-paw with the conversation, so I said – '*Croí an diabhail*, Ned where are you going with the pints or what class of caper is this?'

'Ah lads,' says he, 'have patience with me I have a pledge against drinking in public houses.' Of course as the day wore on he forgot to go out and broke that pledge too!

Ned was married. God help the poor children they were often hungry and the wife was to be pitied. Now it so happened that the wife had an aunt. A pure druidess of a one. She came visiting and she wasn't long in the house when she pointed out to Ned the error of his ways. He had to go down on his knees and promise that he'd give the drink the go-by or she said she'd make a *lúbán* of him, and she would, for she was a fierce major of a woman. She marched him into the convent to Sister Binidict and made him take the teetotaller's pledge.

And to everyone's surprise he kept it – well for a while. One day in town he fell into bad company and broke out. He arrived home paralatic. He had to hold on to the back of a chair in an effort to maintain his relationship with the perpendicular and to make things worse his wife's aunt was there. Did she read him a lesson!

'After all the promises you made,' says she. 'A man with such little respect for his word, not to mind the welfare of his wife and family, could not expect to see the light of heaven! A nice husband! and a nice father. Have you no fear of the hereafter? And what would you do if the Lord called on you this minute.'

'To tell you the truth, auntie,' says Ned, 'I couldn't stir a leg!'

Ned went steady after that – he had to for the wife's aunt came to live in the house with 'em, but even in time she relented a small bit. Ned was allowed to go back to one of his former pledges, a pint a day – no quarts or sweet gallons – just, as the aunt put it, one imperial pint a day. Ned got into the habit of taking the pint about closing time or a little after it, and there is a bit of history attached to that too, and I might as well tell it while I'm at it.

Ned had a white tom cat that used folly him everywhere. He'd go up the stairs after him every night when he was going to bed. Ned'd be tricking with him and they'd have a little boxing match through the banisters of the stairs. When Ned'd take his trousers off and put it on the seat of the chair, the cat'd make a hammock of that until morning. He'd cross the street every night after him and sit on the window-sill of the pub until Ned came out.

The cat was as well known as a bad ha'penny. People passing along the village at night and seeing him sitting on the window-sill of Meskill's pub knew that Ned Connor was inside having his daily imperial, which he never went beyond and his temperence brought him a little prosperity.

You see he had a fine roomy house and the wife encouraged by the aunt began to keep people – turned it into an aiting house.

Two young guards used to have their dinner there. The force was only in its infancy at the time. The guards weren't long coming to the house when they were like one of the family. Yerra, they'd go in and sit in the kitchen, and throw their caps on top of the dresser. In the kitchen they came to know the cat. They came to know too about Ned's habit of going across the road to Meskill's for his daily pint after closing time, and knowing Ned so well they'd never raid the pub while the cat was sitting outside on the window-sill.

Raiding pubs was almost a nightly occurence that time, for the licensing laws were not as liberal then as they are now. The weekly paper'd be full of court cases. I saw it given down myself where a guard at twelve o'clock at night after being given an assurance by the publican that there was no one on the premises, went upstairs, opened the door of a wardrobe and a man fell out. People'd go into an auger hole rather than have their names in the paper!

The guard swore that in another room he found three men sound asleep in a small bed with the clothes up to their chins, the picture of innocence. What they didn't know was that their feet were cocking out at the bottom.

'A wonder they didn't feel the cold!' says the Judge.

'How could they,' said the guard, 'and they having their shoes on!'

But to go back to Ned. I was in Meskill's myself one night when he came in. Even though it was gone closing time there was a big crowd inside. There was something on in the village the same day. I think it was a bull inspection. The publican was in no hurry out with 'em and now that Ned was in, and the cat outside he felt safe ... at least for the length of time it took Ned to down one imperial pint.

The talk was nice an' leisurely and Ned'd be no more than half way down the glass when there was a sharp knock at the front door.

'Open up in the name of the law!'

'*Croí an diabhail*,' says Ned, 'it must be strange guards.

113

Our own lads'd have noticed the cat!'

'Clear,' says the publican, frightened of an endorsement, 'out the back!' as he began to pour drink down the shore. In another second the lights were out, total eclipse, and there was what I can only describe as a stampede towards where we thought the back door should be. We were going into presses and everything. And when we found the door the first of the crowd out were bolting back like a squad of rabbits that'd meet a ferrit in the turn of a burrow! There was another guard at the back gate!

Now, we made for the stairs, and some of us got out the upper window on to the roof of a shed, and the plan was, if our geography was correct, to get down into a neighbour's yard and make good our escape. And do you know what I'm going to say! The corrugated iron roof of a shed on a wet night is an awful slippery place. The legs were taken from under one fellow and he went sliding down and fell ten feet on top of God only knows what! I could not repeat here what he said, and he had hardly himself straightened when another fellow fell on top of him.

Well, there was one huge corporation of a man there – they told me after he was home from South Africa on holidays – and we were all hanging out of him. Blessed hour tonight if the man didn't lose his balance, and crashed on the flat of his back on the roof bringing us all down with him. Such a report! Cows, pigs, geese, all the animals in the vicinity woke up, as we went skeeting down the roof and fell on top of one another into the black hole of Calcutta!

Then you heard the language! Drink lubricates the talking machine – 'twas like Dunkirk! And to make matters worse, whatever way it happened, down into the publican's yard we fell. The guards were there before us, our names were taken, so we had all our work for nothing!

When we came out in the street Ned Connor went straight to the window-sill, but there was no sign of the white cat. He couldn't believe his eyes. Whatever look we gave, there below on the school wall was Ned Connor's white cat holding a loud conversation with a member of his own community, and she seemed to be saying to him, 'Not now-ow-ow. Not now-ow-ow.'

'Well bad manners to you anyway, Pangur Bán!' says Ned rubbing his shins, 'I'd have nearly gone without my imperial pint tonight if I knew you had a date!'

# Tobacco

## Eamon Kelly*

There was a man here near us, a cobbler, and he was full sure that John Bull was a certain rich man living in a big mansion over in London. And when the old age pension came out in 1908, nothing in the world'd convince him, but that John Bull was paying it all out of his own pocket! The cobbler was going around saying, 'He must be rotten with money and all of it he's giving away!'

But to go back to 1908. One comical result of the news that a pension was coming in for everyone over seventy was, that some women aged ten years in one night!

One woman, we all heard of, whenever she'd have a row with the husband she'd grig him with – 'The fooleen I was, a young girl like me, to marry an old lad like you, ten years older than me. Wasting my life on you!' As it turned out she was drawing the pension before him. Or can anyone believe daylight from women! They were quick to take the pension!

But joking apart, it is very hard for us to realise how badly off old people were at that time. You see, they'd have given over their house and land to a son. Of course there used to be an agreement or an understanding that the old couple would remain on in the place and be supported. In return for that support the old man'd work in the fields as long as he was able, and the old woman'd give a hand around the house and mind the children as long as she was able.

Old people could be an asset in the house, and the generations could get along fine together and they did. The one fly, of course, in the ointment, could be the son's wife. A lot depended on her and on her nature. She'd have her own young children to occupy her and as the old people got older and more helpless they might be coming in her way, and

---

* From *In My Father's Time* by Eamon Kelly.

116

relations, as the man said, could get strained! They'd be strangers in her eyes and if she was hard-hearted she'd begrudge 'em the very bite that went into their mouths.

In one house, not a thousand miles from where I'm sitting, they had a bull in the tub; at dinner time the daughter-in-law put a bit of beef the size of a half-crown in the old man's plate. God, it looked miserable alongside a mountain of turnips. He called for more. She gave him another bit of beef the size of a shilling and a big scoop of turnips.

'Gi' me more mate!' says he.

'You've enough,' she told him. 'If you ate any more of it the bull'll be roaring inside you.'

'Why, then,' says he, 'it won't be for the want of turnips!'

I tell you the pension was a blessing to old people. It made 'em independent, although it was only five shillings in 1908, or maybe only half-a-crown. They were able to contribute towards their support, and the man could invest in a half-quarter of tobaccy, and the woman in an ounce of snuff, if she was that way inclined. Bonar Law or Asquith, or whoever brought in that pension should be given a medal – there are statues being put up to men that did nothing!

Prior to the pension there was this old man, and like the story a while ago, he was living with his son and daughter-in-law. They had a rising family and because of that, and the poverty of times and the poorness of the land, they were pulling the devil by the tail. But the daughter-in-law was a big-hearted woman, a good servant, and whatever was going, everyone, including the old man, got his fair share. But she drew the line on that. Not one ha'penny would she spend on tobaccy for him.

And I wouldn't mind but he was a martyr to the pipe. He'd give his right hand from the elbow down, for a smoke. Usedn't he try and cure the leaves of the *cupóg* and smoke it – he used! And he'd smoke white turf. Some brands of that were very hot. He'd have to lie on the bed after with his tongue out trying to cool it!

His eyes used to get watery for the want of a smoke. He'd get so blind walking along the road, he'd be saluting gate piers.

'That you John! Have you any bit of tobaccy!'

Even the bush growing out of the side of the ditch, he'd think it was a saddle horse! *An buile tobac* the old people'd call that form of madness.

The time I'm talking about his eldest grandson was about seven or eight years. He and his grandfather were great friends; they were as thick as a cow and cock of hay. And it used to grieve the little garsún to see his granda suffering for the want of a smoke. Often when the two of 'em would be sitting down together minding the cows out of the rhygrass the young lad'd say:

'Granda! Granda! When I'm big I'm going to get an awful lot of money and what am I going to buy for you?'

'An ounce of tobacco,' the old man'd say. 'You can keep the rest of it for yourself!'

And short as the legs were under the grandson, you'd often see him belting across the fields if he heard a neighbour was at a wake or a funeral, to know would he have even half a pipeful of tobaccy for his granda.

If ever he succeeded in getting a knob of plug, he'd call his granda behind the car-house where there was a seat in the *cúl gháirdín*, and sitting there together he'd watch the old man cut up the tobacco, and then break it with his fingers into *brúscar* in the palm of his left hand, very careful not to let the smallest morsel of it fall on the ground.

Then there'd be a big ceremony preparing the pipe, scraping the inside of it with the knife and turning the ashes into the pipe cover, which'd be made out of a blackening tin. A few handy taps with the handle of the knife on the bottom of the upturned pipe to make sure it was empty. Then he'd put it in his mouth and suck the air through it. A thousand pounds to a penny it would be blocked, so the young lad'd have to go and get a *tráithnín* to act as a *réiteoir*.

He'd watch his granda take the pipe apart at the place where the silvery ferrule was, and run the *tráithnín* through the short stem until it disappeared, and when it came out the other side the fox's tail at the end of the sop'd be as black as the ace of spades – the same as if you pulled a bush through a chimney.

118

Then, after freeing that part of the stem from the ferrule up to the head, his granda'd put the pipe together, put it in his mouth, and this time you could hear air whistling through it. Now, to fill it. The mouth of the pipe'd be put under the palm of the left hand, and with the right forefinger his granda'd coax the tobaccy into the pipe, searching the crevices of his palm and in between his fingers for any stray particles of the precious weed. Then the ashes in the cover'd be spread on top and pressed down, not too hard, with the thumb. Nothing now but to redden it!

He'd have no match of course! Only millionaires had matches that time, so he'd cut a strong twig, bring it to a sharp point with the knife and give it to the grandson. He'd go into the kitchen and spear a half-red coal of fire and bring it out. The old man'd blow the coal to get a little flame. Then he'd put the coal on top of the pipe, maybe shading it with his hat, start to puff and in a few seconds he'd be going like a limekiln. But it would have to get nice and red before he'd put on the cover, and then he was smoking in earnest.

A great look of contentment'd come over his face and the garsún'd smile to see his oul gran' so happy. After the smoke the old man'd be in form to sing a bit of a song, a quiet crónán.

> If all the fair maidens were hareson the mountain,
> Very soon the young men'd get guns and go fowling.
> Tah ral dah ral die do ral rex tee ding tol die day.
>
> If all the fair maidens were blackbirds and thrushes,
> Very soon the young men'd be baiting the bushes.
> Tah ral dah ral die do ral, rex tee ding fol die day.
>
> If all the fair maidens were green rushes growing,
> Very soon the young men'd get scythes and go mowing.
> Tah ral, dah ral die do ral, rex tee ding fol die day.

I don't think people lived as long that time as they do now. Anyway it came to the old man's turn, and he was called away. The children were put up to bed in the loft earlier than usual that evening. The house had to be readied, and provisions got for neighbours and relatives that'd be coming to the wake.

Sometime out in the night the grandson woke up. He thought it strange all that buzz of conversation under him. Then he remembered. It must be the wake. He never saw a wake before. He stole out of the bed and over to the well of the stairs. The kitchen was full. Some people were sitting over to the table drinking tea, a thing he wouldn't get himself only once in a wonder. There was no shortage. Little did the child know that people used to break themselves that time in order to have a good wake.

He could see saucers of snuff going around. Everyone taking a pinch and praying:

'The Lord have mercy on his soul.'

'*Solus na bhflaitheas dúinn go léir.*'

'Amen, a *Thiarna*!,

'He's in heaven anyway.'

'What did he ever do to anyone!'

'All his life trying to make ends meet!'

The next thing he saw was a man going around with a bucket of porter and handing out cups of it. And he said to himself, 'they all liked my granda!' If he only knew, some of 'em hardly knew him.

The place was full of smoke. The child thought the chimney wasn't pulling. Not at all, 'twas tobaccy smoke. The surprise he got to see every man and some of the old women puffing away to their heart's content!

He came down the stairs and moving in and out through the crowd he made off to the room where his granda was laid out. 'Oh God help us poor oul gran. He got so small and so pale!'

The room was full of people too, and he couldn't take his eyes off two men that were there cutting tobaccy and filling it into clay pipes. And looking at all the tobaccy he ran over to the bed:

'Oh granda!' he said, 'isn't it an awful pity you didn't live till the stuff got plentyful.'

# The Drink of Gold

## Kate Ahern[*]

There was a widow-woman one time and her son got married to a nice girl, but the old woman never made any way friendly with the daughter-in-law, and the poor girl was scalded from her, and the old woman taking care not to pretend anything to the son, for fear he would take his wife's part, and the young woman saying nothing for fear she would rise a row between mother and son. Faith, I tell you she had no easy time.

Finally the old woman took some sickness and it was plain that she was not long for this world. And she had a lot of money put aside, all in sovereigns in a bag under her mattress. And what did she decide on doing but to take it to the next world with her, or into the grave with her anyhow, for fear the daughter-in-law would get it. And there was a woman that was a long time a servant girl in the house, minding the old woman. And the old woman told her to get the bag of gold and to put it down in a skillet over the fire and to melt it, so that she could drink it and take it with her. And the servant did not know what to do. Well, the priest came to give the old woman the last sacraments, and the servant girl asked his advice. 'I don't think it is right,' says she, 'for the dying to rob the living. And, anyhow, wouldn't it burn the inside out of her if she drank it? What will I do at all, Father?' 'What you'll do, my good woman,' says he, 'is to put down a couple of pounds of butter and melt it, and give it to her. It will do her no harm, and it will satisfy her. She is wandering a bit in the head, the poor thing. And you'll give the money to the young man and his wife as soon as the old woman is gone.'

And that is what she did. She had to keep re-heating the

---

[*] From *Folktales of the Irish Countryside* by Kevin Danaher.

butter for two or three days, and the old woman trying to swallow it down and it putting *masmas* on her, and she certain that it was the gold. And she died happy, thinking that she had the gold taken from the daughter-in-law. There is no knowing what some people will do, with the dint of meanness and miserliness.

# The Pig-Headed Child

## Kate Ahern*

Long ago, in the bad times, there were hundreds of poor people travelling the roads. Some of them were able to do a day's work or take a job with a farmer, but there were more that weren't able to work, and all they could do was to stretch out their hand for charity at the door. And the one you would pity most of all was the poor woman, a widow maybe, with young children. And it is many a one of that class of a poor person that would be dead long ago, only for the help they got from the houses along the road. And, by the same token, it is often they would get a better welcome at a small farmer's house or at a labourer's cottage than at the big house of rich people.

Well, I often heard a story about one of these poor people, the kind of a story that would frighten you. It seems that there was this poor widow going the road with a lot of children. The youngest one only an infant up in her arms and two more very small ones hanging on to her skirt and two or three more a bit bigger running around her. And the only way she could get the bite and the sup to keep them alive was to stretch out her hand at the door of the houses along the road.

There was a big house in that part of the country, belonging to a big farmer, a sort of a half gentleman. And he would be a decent generous sort of a man only for his wife. She was a devil with a miserly mind and a hungry heart that would not let her stretch out a crust of bread to a poor person and he starving. And the poor people going the road knew very well that it was no use in the world for them to go next or near her door, and, faith and sure, it was far away from her they kept. But one cold winter's day, in the evening with the darkness coming down this poor widow-woman

---

* From *Folktales of the Irish Countryside* by Kevin Danaher.

and her children were passing the big house on the road. And the poor creature didn't know what kind of a house it was, and in with her and the children up the avenue to the door, and they thinking that maybe they would get the night's lodging, to be in out of the cold, as well as a bite for their supper.

The woman of the house was sitting on a big armchair up at the front window, watching out for fear any one of the servants would be a minute idle or for fear a ha'porth of anything would go astray, and she saw the poor woman and the flock of children coming. She called down to the servant at the door. 'What do those dirty people want?' says she. 'It is a poor woman and her children that want some little help, ma'am,' says the servant. 'Tell that sow and her litter that if they are not off my land as quick as they can foot it, it is how I'll set the dogs on them!' And the servant girl couldn't say a word with the fright, but the poor woman heard it well enough. She said nothing, but turned away with the children, God help them, the poor creatures.

But it was always said that you should never liken a Christian to a beast, and signs be on it, it wasn't long until the woman of the house had cause to regret what she said. There was a child expected in the house, and when the child was born, God bless the mark! wasn't it a little girl with a pig's head. And she grew up in the house, and until the day she died they never let her out in dread she would be seen. And she could never talk, only to squeal and grunt like a pig. And she couldn't eat or drink like a Christian either; all she could do was to eat like a pig out of a silver trough they made for her.

# The Proud Girl

## Kate Ahern[*]

A thing that you would often see long ago, and sometimes even still is a girl or a woman walking along with a bucket of water on her head. When I was small every woman in the parish could do it. They used to have a bit of an old stocking and a nice twist of hay inside in it and it turned around for all the world like a black pudding, and they would put that on top of their head to balance the bucket and to save their head. What they had before the zinc buckets and the enamel ones were timber buckets and cans. The can had straight sides and one stave rising up above the others.

I heard a story about a girl who was going to the market one day and she had a fine can of cream on her head. And she walking along the road she was making up in her head what she would do with the money she got for the cream. She was going to buy a setting of eggs and put them to hatch, and then she would have twelve chickens when they came out. And the next year after that there is no knowing the number of fowl she would have. And she was going to have the world and all of the eggs for sale, and plenty of chickens at every fair and market, and she making money hand over fist. And with that big fortune, there would be no bother to her to marry a rich farmer, with the grass of forty cows, maybe. And she would have the finest dresses and coats, and a hat on her head going to mass on Sunday. 'And,' says she to herself, 'there's them that I won't look at, nor on the side of the road they are on, but only to toss my head like this and I passing them out.' And with that she tossed her head, and down with the can of cream on the road. I always heard it said that pride goes before a fall, and isn't that the proof of it?

---

[*] From *Folktales of the Irish Countryside* by Kevin Danaher.

# The Feet-water

## Michael Dawson*

In every house in the country long ago the people of the house would wash their feet, the same as they do now and when you had your feet washed you should always throw out the water, because dirty water should never be kept inside the house during the night. The old people always said that a bad thing might come into the house if the water was kept inside and not thrown out, and they always said, too, that when you were throwing the water out you should say 'Seanchain!' for fear that any poor soul or spirit might be in the way. But that is not here nor there, and I must be getting on with my story.

There was a widow-woman living a long time ago in the east of County Limerick in a lonely sort of a place, and one night when she and her daughter were going to bed, didn't they forget to throw out the feet-water. They weren't long in bed when the knock came to the door, and the voice outside said: 'Key, let us in!' Well, the widow-woman said nothing, and the daughter held her tongue as well. 'Key, let us in,' came the call again, and, faith! this time the key spoke up. 'I can't let you in, and I here tied to the post of the old woman's bed. 'Feet-water, let us in!' says the voice, and with that, the tub of feet-water split and the water flowed around the kitchen, and the door opened and in came three men with bags of wool and three women with spinning wheels, and they sat down around the fire, and the men were taking tons of wool out of the bags, and the little women were spinning it into thread and the men putting the thread back into the bags. And this went on for a couple of hours and the widow-woman and the girl were nearly out of their minds with the fright. But the girl kept a splink of sense about her, and she remembered that there was a wise woman living not

* From *Folktales of the Irish Countryside* by Kevin Danaher.

too far away, and down with her from the room to the kitchen, and she catches up a bucket. 'Ye'll be having a sup of tea, after all the work,' says she, as bold as brass, and out the door with her. They didn't help or hinder her. Off with her to the wise woman, and out with her story. ''Tis a bad case, and 'tis lucky you came to me,' says the wise woman, 'for you might travel far before you'd find one that would save you from them. They are not of this world, but I know where they are from. And this is what you must do,' and she told her what to do. Back with the girl and filled her bucket at the well, and back with her to the house. And just as she was coming over the stile, she flung down the bucket with a bang, and shouted out at the top of her voice: 'There is Sliabh na mBan all on fire!' And the minute they heard it, out with the strange men and women running east in the direction of the mountain. And in with the girl, and she made short work of throwing out the broken tub and putting the bolt and the bar on the door. And herself and her mother went back to bed for themselves.

It was not long until they heard the footsteps in the yard once more, and the voice outside calling out: 'Key, let us in!' And the key answered back: 'I can't let you in. Amn't I after telling you that I'm tied to the post of the old woman's bed?' 'Feet-water, let us in!' says the voice. 'How can I?' says the feet-water, 'and I here on the ground under your feet!' They had every shout and every yell out of them with the dint of the rage, and they not able to get in to the house. But it was idle for them. They had no power to get in when the feet-water was thrown out. And I tell you it was a long time again before the widow-woman or her daughter forgot to throw out the feet-water and tidy the house properly before they went to bed themselves.

# Folktales of the Irish Countryside

## Kevin Danaher

Nowadays there is a whole generation growing up who cannot remember a time when there was no television; and whose parents cannot remember a time when there was no radio and cinema. It is not, therefore, surprising that many of them wonder what people in country places found to do with their time in the winters of long ago. People may blink in astonishment when reminded of the fact that the night was often too short for those past generations of country people, whose own entertainment with singing, music, dancing, cards, indoor games, and storytelling spanned the evenings and into the morning light.

Kevin Danaher remembers forty of the stories that enlivened those past days. Some are stories told by members of his own family; others he took down in his own countryside from the last of the traditional storytellers. Included are stories of ghosts, of wondrous deeds, queer happenings, of the fairies and the great kings of Ireland who had beautiful daughters and many problems.

A homely, heartwarming collection of tales that spring naturally from the heart of the Irish countryside.